A PLAGUE OF MERCIES

Also by Adam Pelzman

The Boy and the Lake

The Papaya King

A Cuban Russian American Love Story
(published by Penguin Random House as *Troika)*

A PLAGUE OF MERCIES

ADAM PELZMAN

JACKSON HEIGHTS PRESS
NEW YORK

A Plague of Mercies © 2023 by Adam Pelzman. All rights reserved.
This is a work of fiction. Names, characters, places, and events are either the product of the author's imagination or are used fictitiously, and any resemblance to actual persons, living or dead, business establishments, events or locales is entirely coincidental.

Published by Jackson Heights Press, New York.

ISBN 978-1-7332585-6-2 (paper)
ISBN 978-1-7332585-7-9 (e-book)
Library of Congress Control Number: 2023906128

Cover design by Andrea Ho

But what does it mean, the plague?

It's life, that's all.

—Albert Camus

There is a woman who lives in a building in New York City,
on the Upper West Side.
A man just a few years older lives in a building across the street.
These two people live at the same elevation,
the same height,
one hundred feet above the pavement,
above the crust of the earth.
They can see into each other's apartments.
Every night before the woman gets into bed
she puts on a threadbare gray shirt.
The shirt is long and sleeveless and extends down to her knees.
She turns off the ceiling light
and then turns on a nightlight near her bed.
The light casts an amber glow reminiscent of a campfire.
The man in the other apartment wonders if the nightlight
is the woman's response to a fear of the dark,
to a threat real or imagined,

an antidote of sorts.
After she turns on the nightlight
she looks briefly through her window.
Perhaps she is reflecting on another day passed.
Perhaps she is considering the quality of her life,
or the quantity that remains.
Perhaps she is scanning the dark street for signs of life,
for hope in any of its many forms.
From her neck she removes a pendant necklace
on which is inscribed an important date.
She places the necklace on the side table
and lowers the blinds
and goes to bed.
When she rises in the morning
she puts on the necklace
and checks to make sure that the clasp
is fastened securely.
She raises the blinds
and looks through her window
as if to make sure that the world is still there,
that it exists and rotates,
that its viscera pump and swell.
She turns her back to the window and makes her bed.

The man across the street in the other apartment is named Gabriel.
He sometimes watches the woman make the bed in the morning.
She makes the bed with precision.
She tucks the sheet into hospital corners,
tosses the pillows
and punches them
and then stacks them at the head of the bed.
She steps back and admires her work.
Sometimes she will lean forward and flatten a crease
or adjust a pillow
and then step back again.
When Gabriel watches her labor over the bedding
he feels somewhat intrusive and disrespectful.
After all,
he believes that she does not know that he is watching her.
Nonetheless he watches her make the bed.
He reasons that her routine brings him some strange comfort
and he excuses his intrusive and disrespectful behavior
with the logic that a person
who engages in intimate domestic activities,
with the blinds open,
either is indifferent to being observed by a stranger
or has a desire to be seen.

The woman is aware that people can see her make the bed.
At times she is indifferent to being observed by a stranger
and at times she has a desire to be seen.
When Gabriel watches her make the bed
he hides behind his drapes
because he does not want her to see him watching her.
(He can see her
but she cannot see him.)
This asymmetry is not lost on the man.
The inequity of this asymmetry is not lost on him.
After the woman makes the bed
she walks into the bathroom
and closes the door
and steps into the shower.
(The man cannot see the woman in the shower
but if he could see her in the shower
he would not watch,
as there are moral limits to his asymmetry.)
She comes out after ten minutes with one towel
around her head like a turban
and the other around her body.
She heats up the electric kettle and makes a cup of tea.
With her towels on

she looks out the window and drinks her tea.
It appears to the man that she is studying the sky
and looking for clues to something.
He imagines that she is wondering
how she has come to live in this mad world,
that she wonders about the state of her life,
whether she has made good decisions or bad.
Perhaps she wonders about what has happened to the baby girl
she placed for adoption so many years ago,
wonders what the girl might look like now.
(The girl would be a teenager.)
She wonders if the girl will ever look for her,
if she will ever again see her daughter.
(The woman signed a form at the time of adoption
and entered her DNA into a database
with the hope that the girl might one day search for her.
The girl has no legal right to search for her biological mother
until she turns eighteen.
She turns eighteen
in fourteen months
and six days.)
Perhaps the woman thinks of nothing
as she gazes out the window.

Perhaps she simply enjoys the feeling of warmth
that emanates from the hot mug
and radiates into the flesh of her palms.
After drinking the hot tea
she readies herself for the workday.
She dresses smartly for the office.
She takes great professional pride in her attire.
Some days she wears a dark suit.
Some days she wears a dark dress.
The man who watches does not know what she does for a living
but he imagines that she is a lawyer
or a banker
or an insurance executive.
Maybe she works for a museum
or a media company.
She often returns to her apartment in the early evening,
sometimes with a girlfriend
and sometimes with a man.
When she comes home with a girlfriend
Gabriel watches them share a bottle of wine.
He watches them talk
or play backgammon
or dance.

When she comes home with a man
they sit on the couch and share a bottle of wine.
They lean close to each other
and speak with a great earnestness that is interrupted
by bursts of gaiety.
After several hours of drinking
and talking
and sporadic gaiety,
the woman lowers the blinds,
leaving Gabriel to imagine what is happening within.
The mornings after she brings a man home
she opens the blinds to reveal
that she is alone.
Gabriel wonders if the man does not stay the night,
or if he does stay the night
but leaves before she raises the blinds.
On those mornings after a man comes over
Gabriel watches her make the bed.
On these mornings,
following the presence of a man,
she strips the bed,
the sheets
and the duvet

and the pillowcases.

She tosses the bedding in the hamper

and opens the window several inches

to allow the fresh air to enter

and expel her memories of the night before.

When Gabriel watches her

he projects all sorts of things onto her that may not be true.

She is named Sophie.

She is smart.

She is funny.

She is compassionate.

She is tortured.

She has beautiful penmanship.

She is restless.

She is brave.

She enjoys tart fruits.

She was orphaned at a young age

but now has a large and loving family.

She is not a smoker

but sneaks an occasional cigarette.

She is principled.

She is prone to bouts of melancholy.

She is creative.

She enjoys Nineteenth Century Russian literature.

She bakes a delicious savory pie.

She represents possibility.

For Gabriel,

the woman across the way represents

Possibility.

There is an old man who lives in the apartment
directly under the woman who makes her bed.
Gabriel watches this man too.
(His asymmetry is applied to people
other than Sophie
but the consequences of these other asymmetries
feel different to Gabriel.
They feel less intrusive,
less disrespectful.)
The man lives alone and has visitors infrequently.
Regardless of the weather or the time of year
the old man wears only boxer shorts
and a short-sleeve shirt
and black socks
when in his apartment.
He drapes a blanket over his shoulders when he is cold.
The skin on his body droops.

His face
and ears
and nose
and lips
and breasts
and stomach
all hang low.
The old man has a tattoo
needled on his right bicep.
The tattoo was once an eagle set against a shield,
but it is now so faded
and pixilated
and hazy
from the passage of time
that one cannot discern what it is.
(What once was clear to this man
is now unclear.)
When he reads a newspaper in his tufted chair
he carefully folds the paper in quarters,
as if he once spent many years
commuting on a train or a bus,
as if he knows how to read a paper
without bothering the stranger

who sits by his side.

For breakfast he has coffee and toast with preserves.

Sometimes he poaches an egg.

Sometimes he eats sugary children's cereal.

After breakfast he takes many pills

for his hypertension

and his cholesterol

and his heart ailment

and his diabetes,

washing them down with orange juice.

For lunch and dinner he makes soup

or a hearty stew

or pasta

in a dented copper pot.

He watches television several hours per day.

Some mornings he watches old cartoons.

He laughs out loud when he watches cartoons.

He shakes his fist in excitement

every time the roadrunner defeats the coyote.

In the evening he often watches sports.

He supports certain teams not because they are good

but because he has a local connection to them,

a historical connection.

These teams are part of his childhood,

as are the cartoons

and the cereal too.

The man never laughs out loud when watching his favorite teams.

Instead he grimaces and shakes his fists in fury.

(How could he not?)

Other than the super who stops by to fix the old toilet

he has not had a visitor in months.

No friends,

no children,

no grandchildren,

no women,

no men.

He has a daughter who lives Upstate

and who rarely visits.

They have a civil relationship,

one that has been devoid of conflict

but also devoid of the affection that he craves.

The old man lives a life of almost incomprehensible solitude

and extreme self-sufficiency.

(He asks for nothing from anyone.)

Directly above him is the woman

who makes the bed each morning.

Their apartments have identical layouts.

Despite their identical layouts

the two apartments do not look alike.

She has furnished her home with modern furniture

and blond woods

and contemporary art

and neutral colors.

His home is filled with old wooden furniture

and worn Persian rugs

and many curios

and a somber autumnal palette.

Hers is clean and bright and minimalist

while his is dark and cluttered.

(They have created different worlds out of identical spaces.)

Sometimes she makes her bed,

the morning light dappling her face,

while he,

directly below her,

separated only by a horizontal slab of concrete,

kneels at the end of his bed

and prays.

He prays for companionship

and for his daughter

and for his deceased wife.
He once prayed that his daughter would call him
but he no longer does.
He has come to accept that his daughter
is not interested in his life,
in his solitude.
For reasons that he does not understand,
but tries to accept,
she is not interested in softening the pain of his loneliness.
Gabriel has watched both of these people for years,
the young woman and the old man.
He feels as if he knows these people.
He wonders how two people could be so oblivious
to the goings-on
above and below.
He wonders about the physical boundaries that separate people
and the infrequency with which unrelated people
of different ages mix.
(In this society,
at this particular point in time,
young and old
are disconnected.)
He wonders if these two people could somehow help each other.

Perhaps the young woman could smile at the old man
and invite him for a walk.
Perhaps she could help relieve his loneliness
by having coffee with him,
by acknowledging his existence,
unlike his daughter
who has remained distant for unexplained reasons.
Perhaps the woman upstairs
could help him understand his daughter
or awaken in him the joy of his youth.
And perhaps the old man could help her too.
Perhaps he could impart some wisdom to her,
wisdom that would help her better navigate this life
and understand the speed with which life passes
and convey to her an urgency
that she may not yet appreciate.
Perhaps he can help her understand the heart of a man.
Gabriel turns off the light and gets into bed.
He glances over to the other side of the bed,
to the void where his former wife once slept.
(He prefers to use the adjective *former*
as it sounds to him gentler
and more respectful

than *ex.*)

He fears that his solitude is as great as the old man's.

He thinks again about the ways that the old man

and the young woman

might help each other.

He fears that

despite their proximity,

despite being separated by only a few inches of concrete,

they will never be of service to each other.

Gabriel thinks about the many simple things

that people could do to enhance their lives,

but for reasons unknown

do not do.

What a waste,

he thinks.

An elderly English couple lives in a low building
that sits across the street from Gabriel's apartment.
Their apartment is approximately fifty feet below his.
They are from Manchester
England.
They are proud Northerners.
They are Mancunians who speak
with a particular accent and dialect,
one that is unique
to their community,
to their upbringing,
to their ancestors
and their socioeconomic class.
These two people spent their childhoods
on the same dreary council estate,
a complex of dilapidated flats
on the outer edge of that industrial city.

They kissed for the first time when they were fourteen
and have been together without interruption
ever since that first kiss.
Gabriel often looks down to them
as they tend to their terrace garden.
The woman focuses her attention on the rose bushes.
She clips off sick canes.
She deadheads the dying flowers
and waters the soil.
The old man often stands quietly
and watches his wife care for the roses,
admiring her skill,
her attention to the smallest details.
The woman keeps a careful eye on her husband,
as he suffers from dementia.
He wanders too close to the edge of the terrace.
(She guides him back to his chair.)
He examines the gardening shears
as if he's unsure of their purpose.
(She gently removes them from his quivering hands.)
She hands him the hose and allows him to water the rose bushes.
He floods the soil.
(She takes the hose from him.)
Gabriel watches the man and the woman sit at an iron table.

There is a tea set on the table.
Gabriel watches the woman
steep the tea until it reaches the proper strength.
She blows on it until it is the right temperature.
(So that her husband's mouth will not be burned.)
She places a sugar cube in his cup and nods to him,
indicating that the tea is ready for him to drink.
The man smiles at his wife
and lifts the cup to his lips.
He nods in gratitude.
Dead good brew,
he says.
Gabriel wonders about the man's dementia,
if it so advanced that he is unaware of his compromised state
and thus no longer lives in fear,
or if he has retained enough of his mental capacity
that he is aware of his deficit
and both mental states thus coexist.
(Gabriel wonders what it must be like for both states to coexist,
to have dementia and to know that you have dementia.
He concludes that coexistence is the worst possible state.)
After the man and the woman finish their tea
she turns on music.
The man and the woman listen to music from their home country,

from their hometown.

They listen to old music from Manchester.

They listen to The Hollies

and The Dakotas

and Herman's Hermits.

The woman taps her foot to the music.

(On beat.)

The man taps his foot to the music.

(Off beat.)

The woman sings all of the words.

The man sings some of the words.

The woman smiles when her husband gets the words right

and she smiles when he gets them wrong.

She reaches across the table and places her hand on top of his.

They turn their faces up to the sky,

to the sun.

Gabriel adores this couple.

He wonders if he will ever again be loved like this man

or this woman.

He wonders if someone will care for him when he is old,

when he has dementia.

Perhaps Gabriel will find a woman like this Mancunian.

Perhaps, perhaps . . .

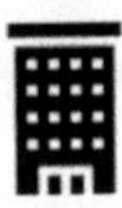

Two young married doctors live together
in the same building as the woman who makes the bed
and the old man who eats cereal and watches cartoons.
These two men are each thirty years old
and have just moved into the building.
When they first moved into the empty apartment
they purchased many things,
including a large television
and a couch
and a coffee table
and paintings for the walls
and rugs
and kitchenware
and so on.
The taller of the two men,
an anesthesiologist,
holds a painting up to the wall

while the shorter man,
an emergency room doctor,
directs him.
Higher,
lower,
right,
left,
no higher,
just a bit to the left.
Perfect.
And then the tall man hangs the painting.
They step back and admire the painting on the wall.
They hug as they admire the painting.
They revel in the home they are creating.
These two people are creating a home,
together.
(What a miracle,
Gabriel thinks,
for two human beings to create a home together.
He cannot believe that it happens with such frequency.)
Gabriel often sees them watching sports in the evening.
They sometimes watch the same sporting event
as the old man in the boxer shorts.

The old man's apartment is two stories higher
and twenty feet to the right.
When the same game is being televised in both apartments
Gabriel might glance
from one to the other,
back and forth.
The timing of the two broadcasts is not perfectly aligned.
The old man sees the action five seconds
before the two young men.
Gabriel watches the old man shake his fist in fury.
He then quickly looks over to the other apartment
to see the two young men shake their fists in similar fury,
five seconds after the old man.
Gabriel wonders how an image could be delayed
when the recipients of that image
are just feet away from each other,
how data can be transmitted to one
faster than the other.
Gabriel turns on his own television
and watches the same game that the others are watching.
He looks across the street.
The old man receives the image first
and then the two men

and then Gabriel.

Gabriel is the last one to get the broadcast,

ten seconds after the old man

and five seconds after the two young men.

Gabriel becomes melancholy.

Since childhood he was always the last to know,

the last to learn that he was being held back in grade school,

the last to learn that his parents were divorcing,

the last to learn that his mother had died,

the last to learn that alcoholism ran in the family.

(Is that why he so enjoyed that first beer at the age of twelve?)

Gabriel turns off his television.

It's only ten seconds,

he assures himself.

I still get it,

like everyone else.

I get the same information as everyone else,

but just a little late.

Gabriel curses his pettiness,

his penchant for victimization,

and in doing so he is able to reframe the broadcast delay.

It occurs to him that maybe he is not the last to know.

Maybe,

he reasons,

the delay gives him the power to see in advance

that which he will soon experience himself.

The ten-second delay allows to him see into the future,

to prepare for what will inevitably occur.

In the television across the street

Gabriel sees his team score a run.

He takes comfort in the idea

that he is in fact

the first to know.

There is a woman who has a grand apartment
just below the two doctors
who receive their broadcast five seconds
after the old man
and five seconds before Gabriel.
She is a socialite,
a hostess,
a patron of the arts,
a widow.
Every Wednesday evening she has people over,
as if she presides over a centuries-old French salon.
On Saturday evenings she hosts a large dinner.
On major holidays she throws boisterous parties.
Sometimes a classical or jazz musician entertains guests,
sometimes a famous writer.
Sometimes an intellectual holds court.
(Gabriel imagines that these intellectuals discuss such things as

resolving conflict in the Middle East
or farming advances in sub-Saharan Africa.)
This socialite is rarely alone.
Gabriel admires the frequency and volume
of the people around her.
He has counted numerous visitors flitting around her apartment.
There are housekeepers
and cooks
and interior designers
and handymen
and personal assistants
and florists
and children
and grandchildren
and friends
and financial advisors.
Gabriel often looks at her apartment.
(Filled with people.)
Then he will look over to the old man's apartment.
(Empty but for the old man.)
He would like to pluck a few people from the socialite's apartment
and deposit them into the home of the old man
so that he has someone to keep him company,

someone with whom to watch cartoons.
With his index finger and thumb pressed close to his right eye
Gabriel pinches a housekeeper
and drops him into the old man's apartment.
He then pinches the head of a violinist
and tosses her into the old man's living room.
He tosses the humans as if he is a giant,
as if these people are ants.
Gabriel thinks about the allocation of people and resources,
how some have too much.
(They often do not realize how much they have.)
And how some have too little.
(They often do not realize how little they have.)
Gabriel theorizes that as a cure for loneliness
resources should be allocated more efficiently,
more equitably.
He gets into bed and turns off the light.
He thinks about this idea of curing loneliness
through the reallocation of people,
perhaps by plucking people from their homes
and moving them elsewhere.
He is not sure how this can work.
From a practical standpoint

he wonders how it can work.
He imagines the small crane that grabs toys
at the carnival.
He recalls a moment from his youth,
with his mother.
She gave him a quarter.
He maneuvered the crane
and grabbed a small toy,
a teddy bear.
How happy he was.
(He kept the teddy bear for many years
and put it in his daughter's crib when she was born.
By that time the bear was missing both eyes
and one paw
and its right arm.)
Gabriel wonders how he can cure loneliness
by moving people around,
from where they are either underappreciated or superfluous
to those places where they are most valued or most needed.
He wonders how he can cure his own loneliness.

The young woman wakes up.

She raises the duvet over the bed and shakes it,

once,

twice,

three times,

until she has it just right.

She punches the pillows,

not in violence but to return them to their proper state.

She arranges them at the top of the bed.

Once she makes the bed to her satisfaction

she walks toward the bathroom.

On the way she glances out the window,

across the street,

to the apartment where the man who watches her lives.

She has been watching him

watching her.

Without the man's knowledge

she has restored symmetry.

She does not know his name.

(Gabriel.)

She thinks that she sees him hiding behind his drapes,

watching her.

She laughs.

She does not feel self-conscious or threatened

by the fact that this man watches her.

She once told a girlfriend that she makes the bed

and that a man watches her from across the way,

from behind her curtains.

The friend was troubled,

disturbed.

That's weird,

she said,

that you're in your nightshirt

and that he watches.

You should report him.

The woman who makes the bed sighed.

She shrugged her shoulders.

Why would I report him?

Gabriel peeks out from behind the drapes

as Sophie crosses the room.

She turns to glance in his direction
and he gasps.
He holds his breath.
He ducks further behind the drapes.
He fears that she has seen him.
(She has.)
He fears that she will consider him a deviant,
that she will lower her blinds while making the bed,
that she might encounter him on the street and reproach him,
that she might *report* him.
Sophie enters the bathroom
and closes the door behind her.
Gabriel wonders if the asymmetry that once favored him
has now been altered.
Perhaps the woman's fleeting glance has created symmetry.
Perhaps this symmetry might relieve him of his shame.
Perhaps the cleansing of shame
might provide him with what he admires most in her,
with what he has projected onto her.
Perhaps this newfound symmetry will give him a sense of
Possibility.

The Mancunians are on the terrace.

The woman wears gardening gloves.

She holds a pair of shears and tends to a rose bush.

Her husband holds a hose.

A stream of water flows from the hose

and douses his feet.

He stands in a puddle of water.

At first his wife does not notice that he has drenched himself.

With a dead flower in her hand

she turns to look at her husband

and recalls the little boy from so many years ago,

from the schoolyard.

He was once a talented athlete.

Rugby and football

and a boxer too.

(She has often wondered if the many blows to his youthful head

have contributed to his dementia.)

She takes the hose from him.

She lifts an old rag

and kneels down

and pats his wet shoes.

One of his shoelaces is untied.

She ties his shoelaces.

For balance the man places his right hand

on his wife's left shoulder.

He strokes her hair.

(He does so for a connection to this woman he loves

but sometimes does not recognize.)

He coughs.

He has been coughing for days now.

His throat hurts.

His wife rises.

She is worried about his cough.

She has worried about him for sixty-eight years.

When he broke his leg.

When he lost his job.

When he developed psoriasis.

When he had an abscess in his jaw.

When he lost his job again.

When he lost their home to the bank.

When he lost his confidence,

his faith.

(He is a resilient man.

He is a quiet man,

a tough man,

a gentle man,

a man who prefers to let others speak.)

The man removes a kerchief from his pocket

and wipes his mouth.

The man sees something in his wife's eyes,

something disturbing.

He has seen this look before.

He cannot remember where or when.

(His mind is disordered.)

He does not want his wife to be frightened.

He wants her to feel safe and secure.

He has a flash of terror.

What will she do

without me,

if I die first.

He coughs.

And what will I do

without her,

if she dies first.

He coughs again

and points to his throat.

Allergies,

he says.

(He still has enough awareness to lie to his wife,

to comfort her.)

She smiles.

She does not believe him,

as he has never suffered from allergies.

She reaches for his hand.

She takes the handkerchief

and in horror she rubs her thumb over the linen,

over tiny specks of bright red blood.

He suppresses a wet cough

and snatches the handkerchief back from his wife.

It's nothing,

he assures her.

(They both know that it's not nothing.)

Gabriel looks down to the street below.

The sun is bright,

searing,

pulsating,

aflame.

His eyes water

and he rubs them.

He scans the busy street.

At the corner newsstand

a young man reviews his lottery tickets.

(The man has hope,

statistically irrational hope.)

There is a cyclist,

a pot-bellied man,

who spits on the ground

and clears his nostrils.

(Gabriel believes that the social contract continues to erode.)

A man walks two dogs,
one large
and powerful
and thick-jawed,
and the other one small
and delicate
and showy.
It appears that the large dog could easily kill its smaller companion.
Gabriel wonders if the small dog fears for its life,
if it is aware of the risk it takes by being so close
to the large hound.
He suspects that the small dog does not understand the risk.
The small dog walks too close to a man
who suffers from obvious and severe mental illness.
The man howls and swings a metal bike chain above his head.
Gabriel wonders if the small dog fears for its life,
if it is aware of the risks it takes by being so close
to the man who swings
a bike chain.
A woman crosses the street below.
She steers clear
of the big dog
and the howling man.

Gabriel recognizes her from her distinctive gait,

her limp,

which is the result of her profession.

She was once a famous athlete,

a tennis player of great renown.

The woman has been sober for decades

and they know each other from the meetings.

(He would like to think of her

as just another drunk in recovery,

and not a celebrity.

He would like to think that he is

above such superficial things.

When he once spoke to her on the street

a fan shrieked upon sight of this woman.

The fan asked her for an autograph.

Gabriel swelled with satisfaction at his association

with this famous person.

Afterward he cursed himself for his pride,

for the value he placed on being in the glow of her halo,

in the proximity of her greatness.

He was disgusted by that part of him,

the shameful reward system

that values optics over substance,

that ego-nourishing reward system.)

The famous retired athlete walks past

a Mexican restaurant on the corner,

which is in the same building

as the old man who watches cartoons

and the young woman who makes her bed

and the socialite

and the two young doctors who have created a home together.

The restaurant is diagonally across the street from the Mancunians.

Gabriel often eats at this restaurant,

which offers delicious and affordable food in a lively atmosphere.

The two owners are childhood friends from Cuernavaca

and they took great pride in designing the space.

For many years they saved money to build the restaurant.

The restaurant was their dream,

now realized.

Gabriel is partial to the pescado frito burrito

and the huevos con nopales.

He loves the glass bottles of cola and orange soda

made with cane sugar.

Several nights per month he dines alone at the restaurant.

Sometimes he brings a book.

Sometimes he dines without a book

and observes the diners and the staff.
Instead of ordering his entire meal at once
he orders one dish at a time
so that he can extend the length of his meal.
He wants the meal to last as long as possible
because he finds comfort in the presence of other people.
(Sitting alone at a restaurant is one of the few times
that he feels connected to other people.)
There is a waitress named Rosa who works the dinner shift.
She is a sizable woman from Honduras,
stocky and strong,
with thick forearms
and dense black eyebrows.
She has a lovely smile and bright green eyes
and she moves through the restaurant
with the ease of a dancer.
She has a husband who is a nurse
in the Bronx.
She has three children,
six,
four
and one.
During the day she works in an office supply store.

Gabriel learned all of this over the course of several months.
After being served three times by the woman he asked,
Where are you from?
He was afraid that such a question would offend her,
that it might imply some difference in status,
that it might question her legitimacy,
her patriotism.
He feared that the question
might imply some xenophobia on his part.
She revealed with pride that she was from a small town
called Rio Esteban,
on the Caribbean coast.
Her father was a fisherman,
her mother a seamstress.
(Both are dead.
One from a car crash
and the other from esophageal cancer.)
Rosa came to the United States when she was sixteen years old.
It was a difficult journey,
she once told Gabriel.
Coyotes,
she said,
are the most vicious people.

They are barely people,

barely human.

She is twenty-eight now.

After a few more visits to the restaurant

he asks,

Do you like working here?

She smiles because he does not understand

the difficulties of her life,

because he is naïve,

because he is kind and earnest.

She smiles because she knows that very few people

have the luxury of working at a place

that they like.

I've got bills to pay,

she says,

but I do like it here.

The staff knows I have kids

and they let me leave early so I can get home to them.

Even though I leave a few minutes early every night

they still give me a full share.

Can you imagine?

A full share of the tips.

They don't have to do it

but they do.

(She places a bottle of orange soda on the table.)

Good people, right?

Gabriel thinks about the goodness of some people

and the cruelty of others.

He thinks about the goodness and the cruelty of a single person,

how those two states often coexist.

Yes,

he says,

good people.

A man begins to visit Sophie several nights per week.

They sit together on the couch

and talk

and laugh

and drink wine

and play backgammon.

He stays over.

Unlike the other men

he is there in the morning when she raises her blinds.

They make the bed together.

(Gabriel watches them make the bed.)

Sophie does not strip the bed

like she used to when a man stayed over.

She tucks in the sheets.

He fluffs the pillows and stacks them.

She eyes a pillow with dissatisfaction,

gives it a punch then replaces it.

The man who has stayed the night notices
that she has corrected his pillow.
They make tea with the electric kettle.
They get dressed in the morning and go off to work.
They leave the apartment at the same time.
Gabriel wonders if they are creating a home together,
like the two young men who hung the painting
and reveled in their collaboration.
The fact that the man stays the night
and in the morning makes the bed with her
gives Gabriel some comfort.
He is happy for her.
He is happy that she has found someone
who shares with her
important values.
The value of a cup of tea.
The value of a tidy bed.

The two young men come home at the end of each day
wearing scrubs.
Given their age Gabriel assumes that the men are residents
who work in one of the many hospitals in the city.
The two men are generally upbeat,
optimistic.
They cook dinners together and watch sports.
They entertain friends in their new apartment.
Their siblings often visit,
as do the parents of the shorter man.
They have each incurred significant student debt
and they adhere to a tight budget in order to pay off their loans.
and to save for the child they would like to have together.
They often dream about having a child together.
They wonder about the logistics of such a thing,
how they would go about having a baby,
the cost,

the impact on their young careers,

their freedom.

They often keep the blinds in their bedroom lowered.

(Unlike the room of the woman who makes her bed

Gabriel rarely sees into their room.)

One evening the blinds are up.

Gabriel watches the two men as they lie in bed.

They are asleep,

holding each other,

clutching

and grasping.

The television is on,

bathing the room in its strange light.

These two men,

these lovers,

these spouses,

have fallen asleep with the television on,

the most simple

and mundane

and beautiful thing.

Gabriel finds comfort in the comfort of others.

These two men.

Sophie and the man who now spends the night.

The Mancunians.

The lives of others inspire him.

The lives of others give him hope.

The man from Manchester has not been on his terrace for days.
His wife spends only brief amounts of time on the terrace.
She cuts the dead wood from the rose bushes,
sprays the buds
and then quickly dashes back inside
to look after her husband.
Today both Mancunians are outside.
It is a sunny day,
warm and breezy,
even nectarous.
The woman leads the man to a chair.
He sits down.
She takes out a blanket and drapes it over his shoulders
and tucks him in
and adjusts the hat on his head so that his ears are covered.
A little sunshine will do you good,
she says.

He appears unwell.

He coughs.

Allergies,

he says.

(They both know that he does not have allergies.)

Want a brew,

she asks.

He nods.

She brings him a cup of tea.

Strong black tea with plenty of sugar,

the way he has always liked it,

since they were children.

She blows on the tea and then holds it up to his lips.

He sips.

He coughs again.

His hands shake.

He runs a fever.

His breathing is strained and shallow.

I feel different,

he says,

a different kind of sick.

She believes that his dementia is speaking.

Don't fret my dear,

she says.

I made an appointment with the doctor.
I'll take you tomorrow,
first thing.
Okay,
he says,
but I think I'm dying.
Don't be silly dear,
she counters.
(Since their wedding day
she has feared the day he would die.)
She holds the tea back up to his lips
but he turns away.
Oh dear,
she says,
don't be so stubborn.
Have some brew
and you'll be right as rain in no time.
He gazes at her.
You'll be right as rain in no time,
she repeats.
She fears that he will not recover.
He fears that she will be alone.

Gabriel marvels at the socialite across the way.

He marvels at the fact that she is rarely alone.

There is always a flurry of activity around her.

A dinner,

a party,

a reading,

a recital,

a rehearsal,

a cleaning-up.

She is always engaged with something or someone.

(Often the woman will speak with one person

while several others wait in line.)

A lady's maid works for her.

(The socialite is an anachronism of sorts.

She has been told that the term *lady's maid* is dated

and considered by many to be offensive,

but she is unapologetic,

not in a defiant or cruel way,

but in a manner that suggests

she just does not understand what the fuss is all about.)

The lady's maid,

the personal assistant,

is a proud and patient woman.

She runs the socialite's bath

and gets her ready for bed

and lays out her nightwear

and straightens up the house.

She is there again in the morning to greet her employer

when she awakens.

She prepares breakfast

and reviews the socialite's schedule.

The socialite has come to rely on the presence and support

of this woman.

(She has become dependent upon this woman,

although her pride prevents her

from admitting this dependence.)

The socialite is only alone while she sleeps.

Gabriel wonders why this woman

requires such a frenzy around her,

why there must be so much activity

at all times.

He recalls the adage about confusing activity with progress,

about not confusing activity with progress,

and he concludes that he too is guilty of confusing the two.

He wonders if this frenetic activity changes her body chemistry,

if it is like a drug,

or alcohol

or sex

or shopping

or gambling

or gossip

or self-pity

or attention

or cutting

or other forms of self-harm.

Gabriel wonders if she gets high from the activity,

if she is addicted.

He wonders if this activity helps her avoid uncomfortable feelings,

and if so what the cause of these uncomfortable feelings might be.

There are a few minutes when she is in bed,

before she falls asleep,

when her assistant is gone.

Gabriel tries to imagine what these few minutes are like

for this woman.

Perhaps they are blissful.

Perhaps they are terrifying.

He wonders if these few minutes could be as terrifying

as the few dark and twisting minutes

before he falls asleep.

For the socialite's sake

he hopes they are not.

The man who stays the night,

who helps Sophie make the bed in the morning,

no longer comes around.

She has been having girlfriends over since he stopped visiting.

They sit on the couch and talk with great earnestness.

They drink wine

but there is no dancing

or backgammon

or laughter.

Sophie cries and curses her propensity to ignore red flags.

The next time a friend comes over

she brings a small red flag on a stick.

She waves the flag in front of Sophie.

To remind you,

she says.

Sophie grabs the flag.

She smiles and waves the flag.

The friend pulls another flag out of her bag,

a small white flag.

To remind you that sometimes surrender is the better path,

the more courageous path,

the friend says.

Through surrender there is strength.

(Sophie thinks about these two flags.

red and white,

danger and surrender,

and how we assign meaning to the most mundane things

and command behavior with them.)

Over time Sophie's sadness is replaced by anger

and her anger is soon replaced by acceptance

and her acceptance by some hazy and fluttering contentment.

Cycles of grief

and all that.

(My life is rich without him she repeats,

a mantra,

My life is rich without him.

I need not define myself by my relationship status.

She finds these recitations

to be trite and distasteful,

yet effective.)

She goes back to her routine of making the bed by herself,

pillows fluffed and centered,

hospital corners at the bottom,

the duvet flattened and straight.

After making the bed she looks out the window.

(Gabriel peers at her from behind the drapes.)

Sophie wonders how she has come to live in this mad world,

about the state of her life,

whether she has made good decisions or bad.

She enjoys the warmth that emanates from a mug of hot tea

and puts on a dark suit

and goes to work.

When she returns in the evening she often cooks herself a meal.

She has been cooking more at home

since the man stopped coming by.

Moroccan vegetable tagine is her favorite.

Tonight three of her girlfriends have come over for dinner.

They were roommates in college.

They cook

and laugh

and drink bottles of wine.

Sophie cracks open the window

and the women share a joint,

passing it from one to the next,

blowing the smoke out the open window.

It is close to midnight.

The four women straighten up the kitchen.

They load the dishwasher

and wash the pots

and clean the countertops.

They hug goodbye

at the end of the evening.

Sophie is alone in the apartment.

She looks around and sits down on the sofa.

She looks out the window,

in Gabriel's direction.

A light is on in his apartment.

She wonders if he is there,

looking,

watching from behind his curtains.

(He is.)

She wonders if she will ever meet him,

if he is a good man,

a decent man.

She suspects that he is weird.

(Why else would he watch her?)

For her,

though,

his weirdness is not disqualifying.

He could be weird yet still be good,

she reasons.

The more she has been hurt

the more hopeful she has become.

Somehow her losses have bred optimism.

She is the rare person who gains optimism

with each loss.

Sophie leans forward and drops her head into her hands.

She is tired,

grateful that she has these friends.

She vows to look for red flags the next time she meets a man.

She vows to look for red flags in other areas of her life as well,

in friendships and in work.

She vows to recognize these warning signs

and to act accordingly.

She lifts the red flag that her friend gave her.

She stands in front of the window.

She looks across the street,

at Gabriel's apartment,

at the man behind the drapes.

She waves the red flag.

She pauses.

Where are you weirdo,

she whispers,

I know you're in there somewhere.

Gabriel stirs.

She waves the red flag again

and sees his drapes move.

Gabriel wonders why this woman waves a red flag.

She watches as the light in his apartment

is turned off.

Gabriel enters a church basement
at five minutes before seven on a Monday evening.
There are about forty people in the room,
young and old,
different races and religions,
a wide range of economic circumstances.
More people will arrive after the meeting starts
and some will leave before the meeting ends.
He has been coming to this room for five years,
since he got sober,
since he gave up
alcohol and drugs.
He first arrived the day after he hit his bottom.
In the early days of his recovery he was convinced
that his drinking had just recently become problematic,
unmanageable.
Just the last few months,

he reasoned.

As time passed,

as he began to recall his old behaviors and attitudes and moods,

he came to realize how his problems had started years earlier,

how he had driven a vehicle while intoxicated hundreds of times

and snorted benzos

and fought in a bar

and got a front tooth knocked out

and had unprotected sex with strangers

and paid for sex

and behaved badly at work

and was once unfaithful to his wife

and isolated from others

and lied

and failed to change his daughter's dirty diaper

and fell off a subway platform

and had strong opinions of other people

and how they should live their lives.

When he drank Gabriel believed that many of his friends

were in the wrong relationships

and had the wrong careers.

What he hated in himself

he assigned to others.

When Gabriel first came into the rooms
he heard stories of people who hit their bottoms
when they killed someone driving drunk
or were fired from a job
or went bankrupt
or were committed to a mental hospital
or robbed a bank.
Gabriel's bottom was different.
His bottom was pedestrian
and unremarkable.
He woke up one morning,
two years after his daughter died
and one year after his wife left,
and looked in the mirror
and saw a man he did not recognize.
He saw dry skin
and red eyes
and a weariness of the soul that foretold oblivion.
He saw a person who could only remember
the worst of his past
and none of the best.
That was enough for him.
Gabriel looks around the room.

He enjoys this meeting,
with its diverse mix of people
who are brought together
by a shared malady.
The literature of this program describes
this phenomenon of people
who normally would not mix.
Gabriel enjoys being among people
who normally would not mix
as it is more interesting to him.
Since he started coming to these meetings
he has made friends with
the famous retired tennis player in whose glow
he regretfully basked,
a firefighter,
two cops,
a politician who resigned in disgrace,
a prostitute,
a high school teacher,
a doorman,
a college professor who is an expert
in Medieval studies and the macabre,
a convicted bank robber

and a bank president.
And they in turn have developed friendships,
relationships,
with Gabriel,
an industrial designer
who creates household items
with a clean and elemental beauty.
(He is noted in his field for having created a corkscrew
that is not only aesthetically exquisite
but that also possesses
a pleasing heft.
His corkscrew has become an iconic instrument
in many homes concerned with such things.
He also designed an axe that won an award
at a lumberjack competition.
The axe's weight distribution is so perfect that it can be thrown
with ease and accuracy.
Of the many objects that he has designed
he is most proud of the axe.)
Gabriel sits down at the back of the room.
The speaker tonight is a young woman,
pretty and smart.
She describes how she *pulled a geographic.*

She moved elsewhere with the hope that she would feel better,

with the hope that she would stop drinking.

Gabriel and the group laugh because a geographic never works.

You end up in a new place

and just keep drinking.

(You cannot escape yourself.)

She describes how she started dating a man

soon after she arrived in this new town.

The boyfriend had one arm and drank a lot.

She notes that he drank too much even before he lost his arm.

The loss of a limb was neither the cause nor the result

of his alcoholism.

She tells a story.

(It is the stories that Gabriel loves most.

The stories keep him from thinking about his own story.)

The woman tells a story about driving with her boyfriend.

He drives and she sits in the passenger seat.

They are both drunk and arguing over something trivial.

Laundry,

she recalls.

He steers the pickup truck with his thighs

and punches her in the face with his right fist.

His *only* fist,

she says both for emphasis
and for comedic effect.
What could be funnier,
she asks,
than a drunk one-armed man
punching his drunk girlfriend in the face
while steering with his legs.
(It is of course only funny
if the woman leaves the relationship safely
and gets sober.
In the absence of that outcome
it is a tragedy.
Comedy and tragedy.
Although comedy and tragedy can coexist,
here they are mutually exclusive.)
After the woman finishes
Gabriel listens to others speak.
They speak of cravings
and dangerous obsessions
(red flags)
and degradations
and gratitude
and acceptance

and surrender

(white flags).

They speak of deaths and other losses,

failures and disappointments of all sorts.

They even talk of successes,

which for many of them is

equally dangerous.

(Both success and failure

threaten their recovery.)

Gabriel does not speak tonight.

He prefers to listen.

He prefers to give others a chance to speak,

the newcomers in particular.

He finds that he now learns more from listening than speaking.

At the end of the meeting the group forms a circle.

They hold hands.

The group says a prayer.

Serenity

and courage

and wisdom.

Gabriel feels protective of this group.

He does not like everyone here.

In fact he dislikes several members of the group,

with their silly airs
and their immodesty
and their predatory behaviors.
(There is one man who slept with several young women,
the most vulnerable women,
who were newly sober,
who were still counting days.
Two men who had spent time in prison
had a frank talk with this man.
They implied violence in the way that only people
who are at peace with violence
can imply violence.
The man stopped sleeping with newcomers.)
Although Gabriel dislikes several people in the room
he nonetheless wants everyone to succeed.
In this room
he roots for the success of even the most irritating people
and he is realistic enough to know that he might irritate others
as much as they irritate him.
Gabriel mouths the final words of the prayer.
He holds hands with the famous tennis player,
on his right,
and a college student,

on his left.

The student is around the age that his daughter would be now

if she were alive.

Gabriel squeezes her hand.

He thinks of his daughter

and extrapolates.

He imagines what she might look like now,

what kind of young woman she might be,

what kind of life she might have.

He goes to a different place,

a beautiful place.

But then he thinks about how a fantasy indulged

and nurtured

and fed

can quickly bleed into agony.

He breathes deeply

and finds himself in a place

that is no longer beautiful.

The meeting ends.

The old man at last wears clothes.

To Gabriel's surprise

he has put on a collared shirt and a pair of khaki pants.

He wears shoes over his black socks.

He darts around the apartment

and straightens up the mess.

He lifts the couch cushions

and hits them with a wooden tennis racquet,

releasing clouds of dust.

He tosses out stacks of old magazines and newspapers

and fills a vase with fresh cut flowers.

He opens the drapes

and with his arms

beckons the sun to enter.

There is a mirror in the foyer.

He observes himself

and flattens his trousers

and adjusts his hair.

He wants to look good for his visitor.

Gabriel watches from across the street.

He has never seen a visitor in the old man's apartment

and he wonders who it might be.

(Perhaps it is the woman from upstairs who makes the bed.)

At the ring of the bell the old man perks up

and dashes to the front door.

He opens it to reveal a woman in her fifties.

She is his daughter.

They have similar frames.

They smile when they see each other

and hug as if they have been apart for many years.

In fact they have not seen each other in eleven months.

She hands him a box of his favorite chocolates,

which are made in the small Upstate town where she lives.

She brings him the same box of chocolate every time she visits.

(He is partial to dark chocolate with sea salt.)

She walks around the apartment as if searching for clues,

mementos perhaps,

objects from her childhood.

She searches for clues to who her father is

and what he has become,

what kind of life he now leads alone

since his wife,

her mother,

died.

She touches the objects that catch her eye

as if to have a connection to them,

to be grounded by them.

She removes an old book from the shelf,

a children's book that she read when she was little.

She is not surprised

that her father still has the book.

She opens it and looks for the inscription on the first page.

She smiles at this recollection of her youth.

She returns the book to the shelf and picks up

a small porcelain figurine

of an angel.

One of the angel's wings is broken.

She runs her finger over the broken wing.

Wasn't this mom's,

she asks.

Yes,

her father says,

it fell off the table and broke a while back.

You can imagine how upset I was.

She loved that little angel you know.

The daughter nods and places the figurine back on the table.

She sure did love that little angel,

she says.

They sit down at the kitchen table.

The man lays out lunch for his daughter.

He pours a glass of ice wine for her and one for himself.

He does not like ice wine

but he knows that his daughter does.

He raises his glass in a toast.

These were your mom's too,

he says,

these gorgeous cut glass cordials we purchased in Prague.

They make beautiful glass you know,

the Czechs.

A toast to you,

my precious daughter.

They clink glasses and each take a sip of the cold sweet wine.

Gabriel watches them eat together.

He watches how they eat together,

how they silently pass platters

and bowls

and serving spoons

across the table.

The old man watches his daughter adoringly.

He takes pride in her accomplishments.

She is a beloved teacher at a rural school

and a fine equestrian.

He recalls her early years with a joyous ache,

how she made silly faces

and studied insects

and read book after book.

He recalls the joy she felt when he bought her a microscope

for her seventh birthday.

He thinks about his dead wife.

Twenty-five years already.

The speed of time staggers him.

To ward off melancholy

he takes a sip of wine.

An hour and a half after she first entered her father's apartment,

eleven months since she last saw him,

the woman rises to leave.

The old man appears wounded

but hides his pain with an affability perfected over many years

of disappointment and solitude.

Father and daughter hug in the living room.

He offers her the figurine,

the angel with the broken wing.

Your mother loved it

and I thought maybe you'd like to have it,

as a reminder of her.

His daughter smiles.

No thanks,

Dad,

you keep it.

She hugs him again and leaves.

Gabriel watches the old man.

The man stands alone in his apartment.

He looks out the window

and watches as his daughter walks up Amsterdam

and then turns the corner.

He returns to the kitchen and cleans up.

He finishes the last few drops of his ice wine.

There's a bit left in his daughter's glass

and he drinks that too.

The act of drinking from his daughter's glass

is an attempt by the old man

to feel closer to his daughter,

to form intimacy

in the absence of intimacy.

He sits down in his tufted chair.

His chest heaves.

He weeps.

He wipes his moist eyes with his hands.

He curses himself for the angel's broken wing.

The man fears that his daughter rejected the figurine

because its wing is chipped.

If only I had been more careful,

he mutters.

(The man does not realize that the woman rejected the figurine

because she lacks sentimentality

and for other reasons that she does not yet understand.)

In frustration he throws the figurine against the wall

and watches it shatter.

If only I had been more careful,

he cries.

If only.

Gabriel watches as the two young doctors arrive home
late at night.
They are tired from a long and difficult shift at the hospital.
One man washes his hands in the kitchen sink
while the other man washes his hands in the bathroom.
They each remove their scrubs
and put on t-shirts and sweatpants.
They soon rejoin each other in the kitchen
where they pick at leftover food,
a discordant mélange of pizza
and Chinese food
and falafel.
The taller man fears that he is running a fever.
His husband places the back of his hand on the man's forehead
and then kisses his cheek.
You feel a little warm to me.
He gets a thermometer and takes his husband's temperature.

100.1

I'm coming down with something,

the taller man says.

My throat's feeling sore

and I've been exhausted all day.

Sit down on the couch and I'll make you some hot water

and lemon

and ginger,

the shorter man says,

and then we can watch the end of the game.

The taller man sits on the couch

and pulls a wool throw over his shoulders.

He turns on the game and is not surprised

to see that his favorite team is losing.

Figures,

he says.

His husband hands him a hot cup.

The man drinks the elixir,

which provides him with some immediate relief.

The two men sit on the couch and root for their team,

curse their team.

(Rooting and cursing can coexist.)

They hold hands.

They have each been sick or suffering
at times during their relationship.
The shorter man had a ruptured appendix and almost died.
He tore his ACL while skiing.
He suffered a months-long depression
after his sister died unexpectedly.
The taller man was wrongly accused of bias at work.
He was distraught that he failed his medical boards
on the first try.
He thought about quitting medicine.
(His husband encouraged him to keep going
and he passed the boards the second time.)
He was mugged and had his orbital bone broken.
His parents reject his choices,
his husband,
his life,
his very existence.
These two men have supported each other
through many challenges.
The shorter man says,
Why don't you get to bed
and see how you feel in the morning.
I'm sure you've just got a little something.

You'll be better in the morning.

He leads his sick husband to the bedroom

and tucks him in.

(Gabriel wonders what it would be like

to have such a devoted partner.

He once had such a partner

but he destroyed the relationship with his drinking

and his resentment

and his cruel and illogical blame.

He has come to believe that these three things,

drinking and resentment and blame,

often go together,

work in concert.

He made amends to her a year after they separated.

She accepted his apology,

forgave him,

but vowed never to speak to him again.

He understood why.

He still understands why.)

The old man is back to walking around in nothing but a t-shirt

and boxers

and black socks.

He eats sugary cereal in the morning.

He makes soup out of a dented copper pot.

He sits on a park bench and watches people pass by.

He reads newspapers and watches sports.

He enjoys an occasional glass of ice wine

to remind him of his daughter's last visit.

He does not know when she will visit again.

He fears that she will never visit again.

His pain is sometimes great,

sometimes tolerable.

Every day he aspires to apply acceptance to his life,

to accept things as they are

and not how he would like them to be.

He once met a man,

a priest,

who believed that complete acceptance

is the highest

and most rewarding

and most difficult form

of human attainment,

a Shangri-La

of the mind and soul.

The old man sits on a park bench

and watches the people

and the trees

and listens to the sounds of the city.

He lives his life.

(Acceptance.)

Sophie has an awful night's sleep.

Her stomach is upset.

She wakes up early

and her sheets are drenched with sweat.

Rather than make the bed

she strips it,

just like she does after a man stays the night.

As she tosses the bedding into the hamper

she wonders if there is a connection between the two,

a connection between men and sickness.

When she is finished she raises the blinds.

The morning sun is too strong for her,

too sharp.

Her sickness has made her sensitive to light.

She lifts her right arm and smells her armpit.

She winces.

I smell sick,

she thinks.

She turns on the water in the shower

so that it is lukewarm.

She steadies herself by leaning against the cool tiled wall

of the shower.

She feels faint.

After she makes the bed and takes a shower

she eats a light breakfast,

a few berries and a half piece of dry toast.

Her gut rumbles

and she gets back into bed

and calls her office

and says she will not be coming in.

There's a dull stabbing pain in her throat.

Sophie reaches for a book on her night table

and accidently knocks over a vase,

which crashes to the floor and shatters.

The vase has neither intrinsic nor sentimental value.

It is cheap and purely decorative.

Still she is upset,

not because she broke the vase

but because her clumsiness amplifies her negative view of herself

and causes her to think that she may be sicker

than she first realized.

The old man in the apartment below hears a noise

and looks up to the ceiling.

(He hears the sound of Sophie's vase hitting the wood floor.)

Sometimes he hears the pit-a-pat of feet from above.

(Sophie and her girlfriends dance.)

Sometimes he hears sharp claps from above.

(On occasion Sophie wears high heels as she leaves the apartment.)

Rather than being irritated by the noises from above

the old man finds comfort in them.

He does not know who lives above,

man or woman,

but he feels as if the person above is in some way

sharing their life with him

through the noises that penetrate his ceiling,

including him in quotidian moments

that have the effect of making him feel less alone.

These noises tether him to another human being,

as did the snoring of his wife

and the sounds of her in the bathroom

and the whistle of the teapot as she stood impatiently over it

and the rasp of her breath in the final days.

The death rattle.

Above,

Sophie gets out of bed

and picks up the pieces of the broken vase.

When she does so

she can hear the muffled sounds of the television

in the old man's apartment beneath her.

She drops the broken pieces in the bin by the side of the bed.

She looks out the window to the street below.

A deliveryman cycles north up Amsterdam.

A woman walks an enormous dog.

A garbage truck idles,

groaning and humming.

Across the street

Gabriel's apartment is dark.

Sophie feels a dull ache

that is more psychic than physical.

She waves in the direction of Gabriel's apartment,

to the man in the shadows,

and lowers her blinds.

The Mancunians are on the terrace again.

The man is seated,

bundled under layers of blankets.

He watches his wife while she deadheads the rose bushes.

He has lost weight since the last time he was on the terrace.

His cough continues,

persistent and wet.

She removes the blankets and leads him to the door.

He is unsteady on his feet.

She places one hand on the small of his back

and with the other grasps his elbow.

She looks at his trembling hands.

The woman takes him around the corner,

to the doctor,

where they test him for influenza and streptococcus.

Both tests are negative.

The doctor listens to his lungs,

which sound clear.

But I'm having trouble breathing,

the man says to the doctor.

Well your lungs sound clear as can be,

the doctor replies,

but your oxygen level is low,

which I don't understand.

I just don't understand.

The doctor gives the man an inhaler

which he hopes will improve the patient's breathing

and increase his oxygen level.

On the way home the wife holds her husband's hand,

clammy and weak.

(Many years ago she admired his hands.

His hands are wide and long,

thick and meaty,

scarred with bruises and cuts.

He has the hands of a working man,

a boxer,

a bare-knuckle fighter,

a dockworker.

His knuckles are so big that the jeweler from Manchester

charged him an extra ten quid for his wedding band.

His wife laughed when she learned that the ring

would be more expensive.

He felt shame.

(The most acute forms of shame

arise for no good reason.)

What if I always hold you back,

he asked.

What if I'm always a burden to you.

She laughed.

Oh dear, oh dear.

She held his hand to her lips

and kissed his big knuckles.)

What do you think I have,

the man asks his wife.

Just a little bug,

she says.

She lies.

She does not know what he has

but she knows that he is dying.

She is sure of it.

She knows that he is dying.

Nothing but a little bug,

she repeats.

He squeezes her hand.

He too knows that he is going to die.

He feels it.

He knows that he will be leaving her soon.

He recalls a moment from their youth.

He sees her on a train platform with her parents.

She wears her finest clothes,

a blue dress and a white hat.

He waves to her

and she waves back.

(He loved her even then.)

And then he forgets that moment

on the train platform.

It is gone,

perhaps forever.

For a moment he forgets where he lives.

Are we in New York,

he wonders.

He sees concern on his wife's face.

Yes just a little bug,

he says.

They walk under a canopy of elms.

How about a brew when we get back,

he asks.

(He has made for her thousands of cups of tea since they met

and she has made thousands for him.

They take equal pleasure,

equal satisfaction,

in giving and receiving.)

She smiles wearily.

Yes I'd love a brew,

she says.

Rosa is at work at the Mexican restaurant that has become

a great success.

People come from all over the city to enjoy their food and drink.

When Gabriel sits down

Rosa brings him a menu.

They are happy to see each other.

They have developed the type of casual relationship

that is defined by modest intimacy

and by healthy distance,

both of which coexist peaceably.

Each time they see each other at the restaurant

they disclose a bit more about their lives.

(She once showed Gabriel a scar on her arm,

the result of an attack.

She was on the verge of telling Gabriel about the attack

but stopped short.

Too personal,

she thought.)

This time she shows him photographs of her family,

of her husband and kids.

They are at a minor league baseball game in Portland

Maine.

The family is standing with the team's mascot,

Slugger the Sea Dog.

Rosa asks Gabriel if he has a wife or a girlfriend

or someone else,

and he says no.

She asks if he has children

and he says no.

(He always struggles with how to answer this question.

He used to have a daughter

but he no longer has a daughter.

He fears that to answer this question,

yes but no more,

might make the other person uncomfortable

or prompt a discussion that might make him uncomfortable.)

No wife,

she asks again.

I'm fine on my own,

he says.

(She doesn't think he's fine.)

Well when you're not fine on your own anymore

I've got a girl for you.

He is embarrassed and says thank you.

He wonders about this woman who Rosa has in mind.

He admits to himself that he is not ready,

that he may never be ready.

What are you drinking today,

she asks.

(She knows that he orders either cola or orange soda.)

Orange soda.

How about you live a little and have a beer tonight.

He wonders if he should reveal more about himself to Rosa.

That he doesn't drink,

for instance.

He recalls the time when a woman broke up with him.

He had disclosed on their first date

that he was an alcoholic

in recovery.

He needed to explain why he wouldn't be sharing

a bottle of wine with her.

Because sharing a bottle of wine on a first date is customary,

the failure to do so is so notable

that it often causes the other person
to sense that perhaps something is not quite right.
They went out on several dates.
Each time he ordered soda or water
and she ordered wine by herself.
(She did not enjoy drinking alone.
She wanted someone to drink with.)
When she ended their short relationship
she said,
I don't have the patience for your baggage.
What baggage,
he asked.
Your drinking,
she said.
But I don't drink.
Okay then your not drinking.
Uh okay.
And not just your drinking or not drinking
or whatever you want to call it,
but your depression too.
On their second date he had explained to the woman
that he was depressed
because his daughter had died.

(She was his only child
and she died of a drug overdose,
an accidental overdose,
when she was fifteen years old.
He fell into a deep depression
and but for a few accidental moments of joy
he has been grieving ever since.
He has suffered a loss from which he believes
he can never recover.
He is damaged.
He believes that he is broken
and unfixable.)
The woman said I am so sorry to hear that
and then broke up with him a few weeks later.
His baggage was too heavy,
too persistent,
for this woman.
How about a beer tonight,
Rosa asks.
He recalls his last drink,
a cold beer on a hot sunny day at Yankee Stadium.
He had words with a Red Sox fan.
The man smacked Gabriel across the face with a cupped hand,

which was a terrible humiliation,

for to be slapped by another man

is worse than being punched.

He smiles at Rosa.

Orange soda please.

For three days Sophie has not made the bed.

Instead she remains in bed.

She wears the same gray shirt.

Her hair is unkempt,

matted and oily.

The woman's cheeks are red.

She no longer stands in front of the window,

studying the sky and looking for clues to her life.

Instead she remains in bed,

making cups of tea from the electric kettle

and moving quickly from bed to bathroom

and slowly from bathroom to bed.

She makes many trips to the bathroom and back,

falling into bed each time she returns.

She appears to be in pain,

weak.

Sometimes she speaks on the phone.

Her throat hurts so much that she can't speak for long.
On the phone she tells her mother that it feels like someone
sticks a knife in her throat.
Her mother asks if she has a fever.
(101.2)
From behind the drapes
Gabriel can see that the woman is sick.
He wishes that the old man who lives below
would bring her a bowl of soup.
If only the old man knew what is happening
just several feet above his head,
if only he knew that a neighbor was sick.
Gabriel wants to scream out to the old man,
Go upstairs and help your neighbor!
Gabriel is concerned that the woman has not had a visitor
since she fell ill.
He thinks about making a sign
and holding it up in his window.
Call me if you need help
He thinks about calling emergency on her behalf
or having some food delivered to her,
perhaps chicken soup with noodles and carrots
or a nutritious juice
or a drink filled with electrolytes.

He fears that anything too spicy or acidic
might further upset her delicate stomach.
Gabriel watches as she stands uneasily.
She walks to the window and stands in front of it.
She looks out and scans the city
before,
below
and above her.
She raises her right arm and rotates her hand counterclockwise,
just the slightest rotation.
Gabriel notices this movement.
He indulges in the impossible fantasy that this movement,
this wave,
was meant for him.
He quickly corrects himself.
I must live in reality.
That is my problem,
I never live in reality.
He glances at the old blanket on his bed,
his daughter's baby blanket.
He recalls the moment when he found his daughter.
She was cold
and blue
and foam formed in the corner of her mouth.

He wailed as he held her.
The only word he could form was *God*,
even though he does not believe in God.
In fact he hates God.
(A self-professed sage,
a seeker,
once told Gabriel that if you hate God
then you must believe in God,
for how can you hate something
that does not exist.
Gabriel bristled at the seeker's logic.)
He repeated the word several hundred times
before the ambulance arrived.
(God.)
There have been a few moments since then
when he has wailed the same way,
with the same cosmic despair,
a primal howl,
a deafening roar.
He does not know what triggers the wailing.
Sometimes it may be triggered by
a girl on the street who looks like his daughter
or a gentle breeze.
or a tap dancer

or a Monet
or the arc of a playground swing
or a Nina Simone song
or the smell of fresh-baked bread
or a junkie in the gutter.
The agony returns without warning
and it rivals in intensity
the agony he experienced when his daughter died.
He in effect re-experiences the past as if it is occurring
for the first time.
He relives his daughter's death.
The smallest things make him relive his daughter's death.
Sophie gazes at Gabriel's apartment,
at a shadow in the darkness of his apartment.
She coughs
and again raises her right hand
and rotates it counter-clockwise just a few degrees.
This motion is intended for Gabriel.
I am here,
it says,
and I see you there,
in the darkness.
The woman lowers the blinds
and gets back into bed.

A party at the socialite's apartment is winding down.
The socialite is radiant both in attire
and in the gracious energy that she emits.
A married couple,
wealthy art collectors,
leave the party a few minutes early because they cough
in a manner that embarrasses them
and makes the other guests uncomfortable.
(Sickness is unseemly.
Decorum has been breached.)
As the guests put on their coats and say goodbye
the socialite's staff begins to clean up the apartment.
After about an hour,
when the apartment is clean
and the socialite is ready for sleep,
her assistant prepares the bed.
When the assistant completes her tasks

she leaves to return to her home in the suburbs
where she will be greeted by her husband and children.
She will return to a boisterous and loving home.
Now alone,
the socialite sits at the vanity and examines herself in the mirror.
She concludes that she is aging well
although she is concerned about the wrinkles
that spring from the corners of her eyes.
In the corner of the mirror is a photograph
from the woman's debutante ball,
from the Pierre Hotel,
when she was nineteen years old.
She lifts the photo and examines her face,
her body.
She traces her fingers over the lines of her sharp jaw.
She moans at the pace of time,
the effects of time.
She looks around her empty bedroom.
From a silver box
she takes a sleeping pill
and swallows it
without water
and with some difficulty.

She stands and walks through the vast and empty apartment
as if she is looking for ghosts,
friendly and garrulous ghosts
with whom she can share a meal
or a funny story.
She opens the refrigerator,
sees nothing of interest
and returns to the bedroom.
She again sits down at the vanity
but this time does not examine herself in the mirror.
Instead she covers her face with her hands.
The silence causes her to experience
an intense and unpleasant emotion.
Her shoulders heave and she cries.
Gabriel watches her cry.
He steps out from behind his drapes and watches her.
He understands why she cries.
He understands why she feels so alone
when there is no one in her home,
when the party stops.
He understands why she entertains so often,
why she remains in motion to defend herself
against feelings of loneliness.

He wishes that the socialite

and the young woman who makes the bed

and the old man who makes soup

and the two young men who together are creating a home

would all gather and share a meal.

And he hopes that they would invite him to join.

Gabriel sits in a church basement.

He is surrounded by drunks,

mostly sober drunks,

alcoholics who do not drink

and who are in recovery.

In the back row is a young woman who is nineteen years old.

She is new to the group

and has been coming for a couple of weeks.

Gabriel recognizes her from an awards show on television.

She is a performer who has been recognized for her great talent

as a singer and dancer.

She has been sober for fifteen days now.

He first saw her months earlier,

when she got thirty days

and then disappeared.

She often cries at the meetings.

Older women sit by her side.

They hug her and offer her tissues.
They speak with her before the meeting
and glare at the men who try to approach her.
After the meetings
these women take her out for coffee or pizza.
Gabriel admires the girl's sobriety,
how despite her renown she shares with the group
the most painful degradations and insecurities.
She has described the time she threw a party at her loft
and felt so detached from the festivities
that she slipped out of the party
and drank alone at a nearby bar.
She returned to her loft only when she was confident
that the party had ended.
She is generally disconnected from the people around her,
adored by many but detached from most.
She cannot connect.
She had three unwanted pregnancies from men she cannot name.
She broke her right kneecap and her left incisor in a drunken fall.
She cancelled two concerts because she was hung over
but blamed her condition on food poisoning.
She has many enablers,
people who benefit from her dependence on them,

people who are more interested in their own proximity

to fame and wealth

than they are in her welfare.

(Gabriel thinks about the people

who provided his daughter with drugs.

He never learned who provided his daughter with drugs,

a failure that he now views

as a blessing.)

Near the end of the meeting the speaker asks

if anyone has a burning desire,

if anyone fears that they may drink if they don't speak.

The young woman sheepishly raises her hand.

She coughs.

I do,

she whispers.

I want to drink.

I want to fucking drink.

I want to drink because I hate myself

and I'm a fuckup

and a loser

and all these people who think I'm great and kiss my ass,

well they don't know shit.

Fuck them.

Many in the room nod because they feel the same way
and the fact that a famous person also feels this way
gives them false comfort.
(Their facts are different than her facts
but the feelings are similar.)
The meeting ends
and people form a large circle in the center of the room
and hold hands in anticipation of prayer.
Gabriel seeks to avoid holding hands with several people
including a man who has coughed throughout the meeting
and a woman who glares icily at him
for reasons he does not understand.
He also seeks to avoid holding hands with the performer
but at first does not know why.
He shuffles in and out of the circle
in an attempt to avoid the young woman,
but he somehow ends up standing next to her.
She reaches for his hand
and he panics.
She looks up and smiles at him.
He still does not hold her hand.
I don't bite,
she says.

She reaches for his hand and completes the circle.
He looks down to their joined hands
and sees that her cuticles are torn and bloody.
His palms sweat
and he is embarrassed.
He hopes that the prayer ends quickly.
Instead the speaker takes a long moment of silence
before commencing.
Gabriel shifts back and forth
from one foot to the other.
The group at last finishes the prayer
and hands are released.
The performer hugs an elderly woman
who has several decades of sobriety.
You did great,
the older woman says.
Gabriel glances again at the young woman's hands,
at her torn and bloody cuticles,
and he comes to understand why she evoked in him
such trepidation.
He aches as a painful memory
struggles for recognition.
When he found his daughter on the floor

he noticed that her cuticles

were torn and bloody.

He thinks about the intense emotional pain,

the terror,

required to cause a person to tear at their own flesh.

He thinks about the intense emotional pain,

the terror,

required to cause death.

The two young doctors are busy preparing their second bedroom.

This room has been empty since the men moved in.

Gabriel eats a delicious pain au chocolat

and watches the men work.

The taller of the two men paints one wall a light pink,

a pale coral perhaps.

The shorter man stares at a manual

and tries with some frustration to assemble a crib.

He can't seem to connect the pieces properly.

He drops a screw several times.

He wipes his wet brow with the palm of his hand.

In the corner of the room there is a changing table,

so new that a price tag still hangs from it.

A few stuffed animals rest on a shelf.

Several boxes of diapers sit in the middle of the room.

Gabriel smiles as he watches these men

and this room

and the expansion of a young family.
It is the type of smile that is triggered by a fond memory.
Gabriel thinks about that hopeful time when he and his wife
prepared a room for their daughter,
one month before she was born.
They too painted the walls pink
and assembled a crib
and adorned the room with stuffed animals and a mobile.
Gabriel and his wife and his daughter
had a beautiful life for many years.
He thinks about the beautiful life
that he and his wife and daughter shared.
They laughed a lot.
They played silly games.
(Hide-and-go-seek was his daughter's favorite until the very end.)
They traveled to fascinating places.
(His daughter was partial to Venice
and his wife loved Cartagena.)
Every August they camped on an island called Monhegan,
off the coast of Maine.
Gabriel's daughter loved to paint
and the stunning light on Monhegan inspired her
as it also inspired Edward Hopper

and Andrew Wyeth.
They would sit by the rugged shoreline
and listen to the water crash against the rocks.
They told stories
by a roaring fire.
He watches the two men in the baby's room
and his smile disappears.
His smile is replaced by a twist of the facial muscles.
The eyes squint,
molars scrape and clench.
These are movements designed to suppress his pain,
the type of facial movements
that are triggered by the most difficult feelings,
feelings of suffocating loss
and despair
and failure,
the failure to do the one thing that a parent must do.
(Protect a child.)
He turns away from the two men who are making a life together.
Their hope is too painful for him,
for what they are building is what he has lost.
He wonders if these two men comprehend
the risk they are taking,

if they understand that one day they must say goodbye,

forever,

and that the pain of their farewell will be inversely correlated

to the joy of their union.

The greater their love,

the greater their pain.

Gabriel prays that these two men might experience a miracle.

A great love without

great pain.

Gabriel looks out the window.

Death has arrived.

Two cars move up Amsterdam,

isolated,

lost,

destined for who knows where.

The few pedestrians walk fast,

heads down,

giving others such a wide berth

that they brush the sides of buildings

and bus stops

and streetlamps.

The city is still,

quiet,

dormant,

torpid.

The city's energy has been tapped,

its force depleted.

The contagion kills not just people

but energy too.

Even the ambulances

are slow

and deliberate

as they glide along the empty streets.

Their shrill sirens clap and echo

against the cold hard husks of the buildings,

their howls and lights unrelenting,

one after another,

a procession of death,

like the waves of an army

facing certain slaughter.

Gabriel looks down and watches the ambulances.

Why do they move so slow,

he wonders.

Death has come to our city,

he thinks.

Death has arrived,

again.

(Gabriel called the ambulance as soon as he found his daughter.

It took twenty-two minutes for the ambulance to arrive

and by then his daughter was dead.
How many times he cursed himself.
I should have carried her to a taxi and taken her myself.
But his wife said,
Wait for the ambulance
it's safer that way.
At the time
he believed that it was a tragic mistake
to have listened to his wife.
He should have taken his baby girl downstairs
and into a cab.
For months Gabriel cursed his wife for waiting.
He could not stop punishing her.
You killed our daughter,
he once fumed while drunk.
He has never forgotten the look on her face when he said that.
He killed their marriage with those few words.
He said something he could not take back.
With those few words
he destroyed a piece of his wife's soul,
destroyed what little was left of her.
With those few words
he also destroyed what little was left of himself.

Even though she knew he was wrong,

she feared that maybe he was right.

Why didn't we take her in a cab,

she wailed to herself

when Gabriel raged drunk,

when their girl's birthday arrived,

when her favorite song played.)

Gabriel looks across the way,

to the apartment of the woman who makes her bed.

She stands at her window and looks down to the street,

to the slow and deliberate ambulances with their piercing howls.

He wonders if she too is concerned by the pace of these vehicles,

if she too understands that time is of the essence,

that death has arrived.

A few minutes of silence pass.

There are no cars on the street.

The sirens have stopped.

There are no flashing lights,

just silence,

stillness.

Gabriel wonders if people have stopped dying for the evening,

if death is taking a break.

He wonders if death is like an organism,

if it tires

and rests

and sleeps

and then comes back rejuvenated.

Ebbs and flows.

The woman across the way lowers her blinds.

Gabriel waves goodnight.

He gazes out the window.

The Mancunians' apartment is dark.

They are asleep,

as is the socialite

and the old man who lives under the woman who makes the bed.

The young doctors are working at the hospital,

drowning in death.

Gabriel feels lonely,

isolated,

disconnected,

solitary.

Untethered.

At last an ambulance crawls uptown

with sirens and lights ablaze.

A lone bicyclist somehow keeps pace with the vehicle.

A bicyclist.

(How is that possible,

Gabriel wonders.)

Hurry,

he screams.

Hurry,

hurry,

please,

Gabriel cries.

He glances at the baby blanket on his bed.

She's going to die,

he mutters.

She's gonna fucking die,

he wails.

(Death is here,

upon us.)

Gabriel has been alone in his apartment for eleven days.
During that time he has not left his home.
Very few people leave their homes.
They leave only to buy food or for an emergency.
The city has become a minimum-security prison of sorts.
He takes the elevator down to the lobby
because he craves human contact.
He is careful not to touch anything with his bare hands.
He pulls his sleeve down over his fingers and presses the button.
Out on the street he squints in the low spring light,
as if he has emerged from a cavern
or a movie theater after a matinee
or from an after-hours bar at the break of day.
The air is dry and cold
and the sky is a wan gray.
His mood is mirrored by the drabness of the sky and the air.
He crosses the street and walks toward the Mexican restaurant

that had become a neighborhood favorite.
He hopes that the restaurant is open,
that it is one of the few that has remained open.
He hopes to see the lovely waitress
who enjoys a minor league baseball game with her family.
He hopes to learn a little bit more about this woman and her life
and to share a bit more of his life with her.
He wishes to be not so alone,
for even the most minor interaction with another human being
might elevate his dark mood.
He approaches the restaurant.
The doors are closed and there is little light inside.
He presses his masked face against the glass door
and looks around.
He sees Rosa,
also masked,
alone in the restaurant.
She is stacking chairs and
removing napkin holders from the tables
and placing them in a box.
She is shutting down the restaurant.
He watches her as he would the woman who makes her bed,
with a sense of distant connection,

tenuous,

fragile,

fleeting,

abstract,

unreal

and yet meaningful.

He admires this woman's struggles,

her courage,

her character.

Gabriel knocks on the window

and the woman looks up.

She takes a step back

and covers her mouth,

even though she is inside

and masked,

and he is outside

and masked.

(Logic dictates that she cannot infect him

and that he cannot infect her.

Among the residents of the city

there are many different understandings of transmission

and these understandings tend to be

inconsistently applied.

People often avoid situations where they are not at risk
and place themselves in situations of great risk.
They cannot be convinced that they have done so.
Panic has set in
and rational thought
is the occasional victim.)
At first she does not recognize him
and she waves in a manner that says,
We're closed,
please leave.
He knocks again
and removes his mask.
He experiences the relief,
the rapture,
of feeling the fresh air against his skin
and of being seen.
She takes a step toward the glass door
and smiles when she sees him.
She too removes her mask.
(They connect.)
When Gabriel sees her face for the first time
he understands that the costs of the contagion
extend far beyond

death and sickness.

Are you okay,

he mouths.

Yes,

she says.

Are you okay,

she asks.

I'm okay thanks.

She points to Gabriel's right.

He takes a step back and sees that there is a small sign

taped to the glass.

The sign indicates that the restaurant is shutting down

for good.

The business cannot survive without customers.

He looks back at the woman and makes an expression of sorrow.

He hopes to convey his sadness that she has lost her job,

that the world has changed.

(He hopes to hide his sadness that his modest relationship

with this woman

has come to an end,

that he will not learn more about her

or her journeys

or her aspirations,

that someone he enjoys speaking with

has been cleaved from his life.)

He wonders if the pain of these small losses

can trigger the pain of the big losses.

In other words,

does the loss of this minor character in his life magnify,

or revisit,

the pain of losing

his daughter?

He reasons that perhaps we relive the agony

of our catastrophic losses each time

a shop closes

or a friend moves away

or a familiar tree is felled by lightning.

Perhaps each minor loss is merely a conduit to our greater losses,

our greater pain.

Perhaps these minor losses imprison us in the past.

(He wonders about the strength of those

who are not tortured by loss.

He wonders about the weakness of those

who are not tortured by loss.)

The woman takes a step closer so that their faces are no more

than two feet apart,

separated by glass.

Rosa knocks on the glass.

You take care,

she says.

He taps on the glass.

You too.

He turns and walks away.

As he walks he thinks about the trajectory of this woman's life,

what will happen to her and her family.

He thinks about the downward trajectory of his own life

and decides to envision a different one for this woman,

a more hopeful arc than his own.

He paints a glorious picture of what lies ahead

for this woman and her family.

Love

and laughter

and health

and prosperity.

Abundance.

He wishes for her the most painful farewells,

forged from the most glorious love.

He imagines for her a beautiful life

and in doing so he remains connected to her

in some vague

but deeply gratifying way.

By assigning to her a life much greater than his own

he has for a brief moment mitigated the pain of his many losses.

The fantasy of another's life soothes the reality of his own.

(The narcotic power of fantasy,

to numb

and distract.)

His fantastical thinking guides him to an image of his daughter.

He imagines what his daughter would be like now,

how she . . .

He gasps.

He thinks again about how a fantasy indulged

and nurtured

and fed

can quickly bleed into agony.

He stops.

The socialite wanders through her empty apartment
at nine on a Saturday evening.
She wears makeup and a cocktail dress.
A smudge of lipstick bleeds out toward her cheek.
Her hair is styled yet slightly disheveled.
The fallboard covers the keys of the idle piano.
The dining room is dark
and the lights that normally illuminate the festive wet bar
are extinguished.
A bowl of oranges sits on the kitchen counter.
The oranges are moldy,
covered in patches of gray-green moss.
The woman pours tepid Sancerre into a crystal goblet
and takes a hearty sip.
She stands in front of the window
and looks west toward the river,
toward New Jersey,

toward some achy nostalgia in the distance.

In her reflection she sees the smudge of stray lipstick

and wipes it off with her thumb.

(Gabriel wonders if she is staring into the distance

or if she is merely using the window as a mirror.)

The discomfort caused by the silence in her home

is too much for her to bear,

so she plays a song that often soothes her.

In a Sentimental Mood

by Ellington and Coltrane.

She returns to the window and looks at herself.

She sways to the slow beat of the music.

She thinks about those risks worth taking

and how they are different for each person.

Some would rather be alone and live quietly.

Not me,

she thinks.

I would rather have everyone around.

The music.

The bubbly.

The friends.

The acquaintances.

The lovely strangers.

The caterers.

The musicians.

The boiled lobster and the filet mignon.

The wine,

the spirits.

She would rather have all of that and risk death

than have none of that and be immortal.

From the silver box on her vanity

she removes three sleeping pills,

two more than usual,

and washes them down with the Sancerre.

The woman who makes her bed is quite sick.

Sophie has been running a fever of over 100 for six straight days.

She eats little and has lost several pounds.

She coughs so frequently

and with such violence

that specks of bright red blood dot her pillowcase.

Gabriel watches her cough

and recalls an old Russian novel he once read.

(A poor woman died of consumption.)

He fears that Sophie will die.

He watches the ambulances move up Amsterdam,

slowly,

leisurely,

in no rush.

They shriek and cleave the otherwise still night.

They move like pompous peacocks

and tear the night apart,

these ambulances.

They carry their precious cargo

with little apparent urgency.

(Gabriel later learns that they drive so slowly

because an arcane and peculiar and illogical law

requires them to do so.)

He extends a hand in Sophie's direction

and touches the glass.

He hopes that she does not have to go to the hospital

for it is there that people seem to die.

Those who avoid the hospital can live.

Those who must go seem destined to die.

There is a hospital in Queens where everyone dies.

This hospital has become a death mill.

Please don't go to Queens,

he thinks.

Please God don't go to Queens.

Gabriel sits on his bed.

He is restless

and frightened.

He feels powerless.

(He has felt this way without relief since his daughter died

and his wife left.

He has seen no evidence that he can influence
anyone or anything.
In fact never in his life has he been able to convince someone
to think or act differently.)
Gabriel watches Sophie from his bed.
When he watches her from his bed he feels even more shame
than he does when he watches from behind the drapes.
Sophie coughs with such force that she hits her forehead
on the side table.
Gabriel leaps up,
alarmed and terrified.
He fears that she will die tonight.
He looks around his room.
He steps into his closet and removes a white t-shirt.
He grabs a marker from his desk and writes on the shirt.
Do you need help?
I can help
He stands in front of the window.
He does not hide behind the blinds.
He presses the shirt against the window
so that the words face Sophie.
Do you need help?
I can help

He waits for her to see him,

to see his message.

Given the distance and the darkness

it is impossible for her to read the words.

He waits as she coughs.

She does not look up to see him.

Here here,

he screams.

Look over here please.

She pulls the covers up over her shoulders

and turns off the light.

An ambulance,

a deathmobile with pretty lights,

ambles up Amsterdam.

He glares at the ambulance

Stay away,

he warns.

(He thinks about the twenty-two minutes

that passed before the ambulance

came for his daughter.)

He shakes his fist at the ambulance.

Stay away from her.

The ambulance passes

and continues up Amsterdam

and disappears

into the night.

The Mancunians are on the terrace.
They tend to their rose bushes
and read the paper
and play with the Welsh springer spaniel puppy
they recently acquired.
(They have owned six Welsh springer spaniel puppies
since they first married,
but never more than one at the same time.
They can measure the length of their relationship
by the life span of a dog.
Sometimes they acquired a dog
when their lives were filled with great hope,
and sometimes when their lives were filled
with fear and uncertainty.)
The dynamic between the Mancunians has changed in a way
that causes great concern for both of them.
She is acutely aware of the changes.

He has only a faint sense of the changes
but feels something in his core that terrifies him.
He knows without knowing.
The old man who was once a boxer
and who now has dementia,
and who coughed with abandon
on the way home from the doctor,
has recovered from his illness.
Despite his old age and cognitive decline
he has the muscles and bones of an athlete.
The lungs too.
Would take an act of God to kill me off,
he once crowed after getting hit by a motorcycle
and walking away.
He holds his wife's clammy hand.
She has been running a fever for several days.
Her throat is sore,
raw.
The man makes her hot water with honey and turmeric.
When he once suffered from the flu as a child in Manchester,
his Indian neighbor gave him this same mixture.
(Where were my parents when I fell ill
and this woman helped me,

he once wondered

but never asked.

Why did this woman from Chennai look after me

when my parents did not?)

His wife coughs.

She gasps.

His father worked the mines

and he recalls the old man's raspy wheeze and soot-filled scars.

He understands what her breathing means.

I need to go to hospital,

she says.

She knows what this means.

No,

he says,

you need to stay here and get better.

She strokes his hand.

There's no getting better here,

she says.

He kisses her on the forehead.

He pulls back and looks at her.

His lips tremble

and quiver.

His mind works

but it does not work.

She understands that her worst fears are being realized,

that he will outlive her,

that she will die first,

that he will be left to fend for himself,

that her dear man,

Patrick,

will have to live with only half a mind

and no one to love him

or guide him

or feed him

or walk with him

or reassure him

or hold him

or help him prune the rose bushes.

There will be no one there to comfort him

when his night terrors tear him from sleep

and no one left to soothe him when he forgets.

He fears everything she fears but cannot express himself.

He's a boxer,

a stoic,

a Northerner.

He is gutted,

destroyed.

He reaches for her hand.

Come dear,

he says,

let's pack a bag and get you to hospital.

They'll make you good as new.

He starts to walk in the wrong direction

and she steers him to the door.

She smiles.

Yes dear,

she says,

it's time we go.

The two doctors return from work and enter their apartment.
They appear to be forlorn,
grief-stricken.
In the foyer they disrobe down to their underwear
and toss their dirty clothes onto the floor,
in a pile.
The shorter of the two men
places the clothes in a plastic bag
and carries the bag down the hallway,
to the other side of the apartment,
where he drops the clothes into the washing machine.
(Gabriel notices the two men remove and wash their clothes
and he resolves to do the same
when he next goes outdoors and returns to his apartment.
He reasons that these two physicians
are privy to information about the contagion
that he is not.

The idea that the microbe might live on clothing,
and for more than just a few seconds,
terrifies him.)
The two doctors wash up and meet in the nursery,
in the room they have prepared for their child.
The taller of the two men sits on the floor
in the middle of the room.
He drops his head into his hands.
He pulls at his hair.
He stares at a photograph of an ultrasound.
The shorter of the two men stands over the crib with a screwdriver.
He removes screws and pieces of the crib.
He disassembles the crib
and stacks the pieces on the floor.
The two men do not speak to each other.
At this moment there is little to say.
They have spent hundreds of hours and most of their savings
to have a child.
For several years they have dreamed of having a child together,
of being parents,
of creating a family.
The woman who carried their child was a friend from college.
At first she was uncomfortable with the idea of being a vessel

to produce a baby for someone else,

but then she became empowered by the idea of being a vessel

to produce a baby for someone else.

(I have agency and autonomy,

she reasoned.)

The men knew there was a problem when the woman called

to say that she was ill,

that she had a fucked-up weird-ass kind of flu.

(Her words.)

She said she'd been to the obstetrician,

who said not to worry

and to stay hydrated.

But after a week of fever and aches

and the loss of taste

she went back to the doctor,

who performed another ultrasound

and saw a serious problem.

That was the end of the woman's pregnancy.

(She wept in a manner that surprised her,

violent and unrelenting.)

The men leave the nursery.

They move into the living room and sit on the couch.

They drink beer and watch their favorite team on television.

There are no fans in the stadium.

Just cardboard cutouts

of random people

and dogs

and celebrities

and cartoon characters.

Bizarre,

they think.

Fake crowd noise is pumped through the television.

Their favorite team often disappoints.

Their team bats in the bottom of the ninth

and is down by one run.

The bases are loaded with two outs.

A walk will tie the game

and a hit will win the game.

The tall man asks,

Any chance we win the game?

The shorter man smiles knowingly and takes a sip of beer.

Not likely,

he says.

The batter swings and strikes out.

(A few seconds earlier the same batter swung and struck out

on the old man's television.

A few seconds later the same batter will swing and strike out
on Gabriel's television.)
The tall man turns off the television.
They finish their beers
and walk toward their bedroom.
On the way they glance into the dark room
that was destined to be a nursery
but is now a reminder of their loss.
Gabriel wonders how these two men feel,
how it feels to say farewell to someone you love
but have never met.
(He once read a book by an accomplished therapist
who wrote about a concept called
ambiguous loss,
when we experience a terrible loss but for some reason
it remains open,
unresolved.
A loved one is missing at war
but not reported dead.
A friend is addicted to drugs,
distant and unavailable.
A parent has dementia.
Perhaps we suffer from some intergenerational trauma.

We have a nagging sense that something's not right with us
but we can't point to the proximate cause
because it happened a hundred years ago.
It's real
but it's not provable,
and because it's not provable,
it's difficult to detect
and hard to treat
and chronic.)
Gabriel imagines that the pain of such a farewell,
saying goodbye to a child who was never born,
can be as exquisite as the pain of saying goodbye
to someone you've known for decades.
An ambulance howls up Amsterdam,
slow and steady.
Behind the ambulance is a bus with no passengers,
a zombie bus.
Gabriel stares at the bus.
The driver pauses at a stop
even though there are no passengers in the bus
and no one waits at the stop.
The driver opens the doors,
front and rear.

He waits a few seconds before closing the doors with a hiss
and then continues his quiet journey uptown.
Gabriel wonders about the things we do out of habit or ritual,
things like putting a candle in a cupcake on his daughter's birthday
every year when she was alive
and every year since she died.
Perhaps there exists some comfort in the ritual,
the repetition,
the thump
thump
thump.
(The opening and closing of the bus doors.)
Perhaps there exists in these rote behaviors
some tether to the past
and some hope for the future.
Perhaps, perhaps . . .

The old man who wears boxer shorts and makes soup
sits at his kitchen table.
He flips through a photograph album that contains
pictures of his daughter and his dead wife.
He pauses at a photograph that moves him.
His wife stands by a hotel pool in Miami Beach.
She wears a one-piece bathing suit
that has a large silk daffodil on the shoulder strap.
In the background there are palm trees
and fake camels
and fake pyramids.
Over his wife's right shoulder is a sliver of ocean,
a brilliant blue.
There is a tanker on the horizon
and the partial wing of a seagull
can be seen in the upper right corner of the photograph.
She holds a large glass,

a tropical drink of some sort.

A blue plastic monkey hangs from the lip of the glass.

and an orange slice drifts on top.

(He smiles when he recalls how she loved

fruity alcoholic drinks by the pool.)

This was the last day of their honeymoon.

The old man experiences a pang of something,

nostalgia perhaps,

or maybe a pang of joy reappearing years later,

when it has assumed the properties of pain.

(Joy can be experienced as pain

and pain can be experienced as joy,

often without awareness.)

His pot of soup simmers on the stove.

Tiny geysers of broth leap out of the pot and spackle the counter.

The old man rises

and turns off the flame.

He sits back down

and reexamines the photograph.

Her auburn hair.

Her narrow shoulders.

The birthmark on her left shoulder.

Her pearl earrings.

Her engagement ring,

a thin sterling band.

Her wedding ring

with the tiniest diamond.

Her smile.

(He adored her crooked teeth.)

His hands shake.

He feels hot,

dizzy,

a bit drowsy.

He closes the picture album.

He experiences no joy,

only pain.

He stands and returns to the kitchen.

His apartment is quiet.

He is poised to pour soup into a bowl when he hears a loud sound directly above him,

a thud so loud that it rattles the plates in his cabinet.

He listens for something else,

another sound perhaps,

some sign that nothing terrible or dangerous has happened.

He hears nothing.

After a minute or so he pours the soup into the bowl.

He sits down at the table
and thinks about his wife,
how she was accepting of his limitations,
how she recognized his character in the very few words he spoke.
(She once said he doesn't talk much
but when he does there's often a pearl in there.)
He thinks about how she never pressured him to be
more interesting
or successful
or talkative
or funny
or wealthy
or well-dressed
or ambitious
or educated
or sophisticated
or cultured.
She loved him for his outward simplicity
which masked his inner complexity.
She loved him for his decency,
for the way he treated her.
(He always believed that she could have done much better
and feared that she would one day leave him

for someone better.

She would not leave him

under any circumstances.)

The old man looks up to the ceiling.

As he wonders what could have caused that loud thump above,

Sophie lies unconscious on the floor of her kitchen.

Sophie takes a long hot shower
which in her febrile state
causes her to feel light-headed.
She goes to the kitchen to get a glass of water
and steadies herself by placing her hand on the counter
and then without even the slightest warning
she faints.
Sophie lies on the floor of her kitchen.
Her head is bruised
and her elbow is bleeding
and she remains unconscious for five or ten seconds.
When she comes to,
she looks around the kitchen.
She touches her fingertips to her bloody elbow
and stares at her fingers as if she does not comprehend
what has happened.
She touches the tip of her bloody middle finger to her tongue.

Her blood has a bitter metallic taste.

She holds on to a chair and with some difficulty rises to her feet.

As she rises

the chair topples to the floor.

From the freezer

she removes a handful of ice

and drops it into a handcloth.

She presses it to her forehead

and then to her elbow.

The old man below stares up at his ceiling.

He listens for another loud thud

but hears nothing.

He shrugs his shoulders

and pours his soup into a bowl.

Sophie staggers to her bed.

She drops to the mattress and falls asleep.

Several minutes after she has gotten into bed

Gabriel approaches his bedroom window

and looks at Sophie's apartment,

which is dark

except for the nightlight that casts an amber glow.

He is comforted to see that she is asleep.

He does not know that she has fallen and hurt herself.

He experiences the ill-founded satisfaction,
the relief,
that one feels when they believe
that the people they love are safe.
(He has come to adore a woman he does not know
because he has assigned to her a number of
noble traits and tantalizing eccentricities
that have the effect of constructing
a human being,
the idea of a human being,
who might save him from a pain that has been persistent
since his life was ravaged by loss.
He has in effect manufactured medicine through a combination
of hopeful fantasy
and the repetition and refinement of that fantasy.)
Gabriel gets into bed.
He closes his eyes
and imagines his daughter.
He imagines his former wife.
He imagines running into Sophie,
the woman who makes her bed,
after the plague has ended,
when life has returned,

when a way of life has returned.

He imagines approaching her on a sunny day,

when the streets are filled with people and joy,

celebrating their lives

and their freedom.

Hello,

he says,

I know you from the window,

from across the street.

I know you too,

she might say,

you're the man behind the drapes.

Gabriel smiles.

Perhaps we can go for a walk or an ice cream,

he suggests.

(She smiles.)

Gabriel sleeps.

Gabriel looks at his watch and is shocked
that it is eight in the evening,
that night has arrived with supernatural speed,
that another day has passed,
surrendering its light to some dark and great force.
Other than surviving another day
he has accomplished nothing.
He does not know what day of the week it is,
whether it is a weekday
or the weekend.
He does not know the date
and for a moment cannot recall even the month.
Gabriel feels a crushing weight on his chest
and fears that he has lost the grounding solace of time,
of increments of time,
of temporal structure
and repetition.

Time passes,

yet he can no longer measure it.

Time is no longer linear,

measurable.

Gabriel can no longer break his life down into packets of time.

He is floating,

spiraling.

He looks out the window,

to the desolate streets below.

He thinks about time,

about the passage of time.

He wonders if something has happened to time

since the plague arrived.

He wonders if time has been corrupted

and mutated

and twisted

and stretched.

(Yes it has.

The contagion has done something to time,

something strange,

metaphysical.)

The distinctions between times of the day

have been extinguished.

The distinctions between days of the week

have been extinguished.

The distinctions between months and years and centuries

have been extinguished.

There are no more eras or epochs.

Gabriel fears that there is now one enormous

monolithic

void-like

mass of time

that cannot be sliced

or divided

or measured.

Time now folds back on itself.

He fears looking at the mirror

and seeing an old man,

decades older than the last man he saw in the mirror,

or even worse,

seeing instead a much younger man,

seeing himself as a child.

He glances at a photograph of his daughter

and shakes with fear.

He fears that this thing with time,

with time disappearing,

will somehow negate the anniversaries,
not just of his achievements
and victories
and rewards
and blessings,
but of his losses
and failures
and agonies too.
He fears that this temporal monolith,
this savage devourer of time,
will turn his clear and definitive losses
into something hazy and amorphous,
ambiguous.
Gabriel trembles at the thought of ambiguity,
at the absence of certainty.
He thinks about the two young doctors
who lost a child
they never met.
He wants to grieve with certainty.
He always wants to remember the exact moments of his losses.
He wants to remember where he was,
the day of the week,
the weather,

the smell in the room,

the clothing he wore,

and on and on.

He steps behind the blinds and peers out.

He sees the woman who makes the bed.

Sophie appears stronger,

more active.

She heals.

Thank God,

he thinks.

(He does not believe in God.

He believes that he does not believe in God.

He may be mistaken.)

Sophie approaches her window

and looks at Gabriel

and waves.

He covers his face with the drapes.

He stays hidden for some period of time.

He does not know how much time passes.

(The monolith is at work,

corrupting and twisting time.)

He feels consumed by some limitless and inky darkness.

He struggles to breathe,

to move.

He fears that only some bold action

can restore his breath.

Gabriel steps out from behind the drapes

and reveals himself before the large window.

He exhales.

He breathes.

Sophie looks in his direction.

He lifts his arm

and waves.

I'm here,

he seems to be saying,

right here.

Sophie waves.

I'm here too,

she signals.

I exist

and you exist.

(Gabriel, you exist.)

Death surrounds us

but we exist.

Gabriel checks his watch.

He wants to remember the exact moment

that this exchange occurs.

(Three minutes past midnight.)

He rages against the monolith,

against the destruction of time,

against the ambiguity of loss.

He looks back to Sophie.

She waves goodnight

and turns off her bedroom light.

Gabriel exhales.

He writes the time on a piece of paper.

He wants to remember.

He desires certainty.

In these most uncertain of times

he craves certainty.

The old man who lives beneath the woman who makes her bed

sits at the kitchen table

and eats breakfast.

He eats porridge out of a chipped ceramic bowl.

The television is on

and he watches cartoons.

The volume is so loud that Sophie,

above,

can hear the television's muffled sounds.

The man laughs when a talking duck

slaps a talking pig.

He laughs when a bipedal rabbit

crashes a car.

Gabriel watches the man watch cartoons

and wonders why a grown man watches cartoons.

Gabriel has not watched a cartoon,

without a child present,

in at least thirty years.

When he sees the joy that cartoons give the old man

he decides to turn on the same channel.

(Maybe the old man knows something that he

does not.)

Gabriel receives the broadcast a few seconds after the old man.

A rabbit in a dress punches

a plump rooster wearing a top hat.

Gabriel laughs as if he has just seen the most hilarious thing.

The distorter of time,

the void-like monolith

that causes time to fold back on itself,

has caused in Gabriel a regression,

a transport to his childhood

that in turn causes

him to enjoy the sight

of anthropomorphized animals

engaging in violent high jinks.

The socialite is in her bedroom in her empty apartment.

She sits at the mirrored vanity

and examines the lines on her face,

the elasticity of her neck,

the slackening of her ear lobes.

Lined up on the vanity are dozens of bottles.

Perfumes and room sprays,

body oils and lotions,

makeup and hair products.

She stares at the mirror

but does not like what she sees.

She has not had a visitor in three months.

(Since death arrived.)

She has not socialized with a single person during that time

and has spoken briefly on the phone with only a few people.

She has not hosted a party

or a dinner

or a music recital
or a poetry reading.
For three months there has been no flurry of activity
and the social energy that used to sustain her and drive her,
that pumped through her body
and provided her with the pep to get through her days,
that energy no longer exists.
She can no longer rely on the constant buzz to elevate her spirits,
to sustain her sense of worth,
to shield her from the boredom of solitude.
She wonders about her identity,
whether she is an interesting and popular woman
who happens to throw parties
or whether she is a rather ordinary woman
who throws interesting and popular parties.
She prefers the former,
fears the latter,
but accepts either.
She turns on her computer and sees that a friend,
another socialite who operates in an elevated stratum,
has invited her to a cocktail party.
How delightful,
she thinks.

She continues to read the invitation
only to see that this party is in fact
a virtual cocktail party.
Make your favorite drink and dial in,
the invitation reads.
She wonders what could be lonelier than to be with people
but at the same time
not to be with those people.
(These two states cannot coexist.)
With a few keystrokes she declines the invitation.
She declines with gratitude and appreciation.
She declines with gratitude and appreciation
in order to preserve her social standing
and to insure future invitations.
Over my dead body,
she mumbles.
The socialite opens a sterling pill box
and removes three sleeping pills,
two more than prescribed.
She washes them down with a glass of wine
and gets under the covers.
The wine and pills soon cause her to feel a bit numb.
She enjoys the feeling.

She turns on the television,

a comedy,

and listens to the noise

and the laugh track,

and she watches the actors move about the screen.

The noise and the laugh track and the movement

give her comfort.

Gabriel turns on his computer and dials into a meeting.

On the screen there are dozens of small squares,

each one filled with the face of someone he knows.

There is the famous retired tennis player.

The young woman who is a singer and performer.

The bank robber.

The bank president.

The bouncer.

The tattoo artist.

The prostitute.

The bankruptcy attorney.

The Orthodox rabbi.

(People who normally would not mix.)

For the first time he can see many of them in their homes.

There are some who live in modest apartments

and some who live in opulent ones

and some who have positioned their cameras

so that it is impossible
to determine much at all about their homes.
There are the fortunate few who dial in from their country houses,
trees swaying in the background
or waves crashing in the near distance.
He is surprised by the homes of many
and takes note of the fact that in his life he has made
many assumptions about many people
and that most of those assumptions
have been incorrect.
He has not seen these people in person for many months
and he is happy to see them now.
The meeting follows the same format as an in-person meeting
but there is a subtle shift in energy,
a shift in focus,
that Gabriel at first does not recognize.
As the meeting progresses
he begins to appreciate what has changed,
how the digital experience has altered the way
that this group of drunks interacts,
communicates,
connects.
Gabriel first appreciates that things are different

when he sees himself on the screen.
Do I really look like that,
he wonders.
(Yes he does.)
What startles him most is not his appearance
but rather the perspective of his appearance,
for what he sees is not a reflected duplication
that a mirror would present,
a reversed image of his face,
but instead an image of his face
that another human being would see
when looking at him.
What he sees is now what everyone else sees.
His nose turns the wrong way,
right and not left.
The scar on his forehead stretches out in the opposite direction
and he wonders how it is possible that a person
can have an understanding of their own face that is so inaccurate.
He wonders how a person cannot know what they look like.
So troubled is he by this shift in his appearance
that he pays little attention to the others in the meeting.
Their mouths move but he does not listen.
He instead stares at his face and tries to figure out

who he really is.

A man's cry of pain pulls Gabriel out of his self-absorption.

(The man has just lost job and has no savings.)

Gabriel knows this man and has affection for him.

He wants to hear what this man has to say,

to grant him the respect of listening to his pain.

Gabriel changes the settings on the screen

so that others can still see him

but so that he cannot see himself.

He is relieved to not look at this image of his face.

He scans the screen and looks at the many people.

He makes assumptions about some of them

and projects traits and qualities on to others.

He looks at them,

he studies them,

as if he is gazing at the woman who makes her bed

and the old man who makes soup out of a copper pot

and the lonely socialite

and the doctors

and the Mancunians.

He looks at the small squares on the screen

as if he is looking through the windows of his neighbors.

The young woman,

the famous performer,

begins to speak.

She tells a story about a music producer who gave her drugs

and tried to exploit her.

Fuck that motherfucker,

she says.

Many in the meeting laugh in appreciation,

as she is getting stronger.

At this moment a stranger dials in

and enters the meeting.

The man is new to this meeting.

(All are welcome.)

He is wearing a cap and a surgical mask.

He starts to scream at the performer,

at this courageous young woman who seeks safety

among other like-minded people

in this virtual room.

The stranger says cruel and degrading things to the young woman,

He says things that are abhorrent and vile,

disrespectful.

(Sexual in nature.)

The young woman covers her face with her hands.

She cries.

If this were a meeting in a church basement
several women would rush to her aid and comfort her
and several men would physically remove the stranger,
but in this virtual meeting
there is no physical reaction to the abuse.
The meeting administrator quickly disconnects
the intruder from the meeting,
but the damage is done.
The young woman is distraught.
She presses a button on her computer
and she is gone.
She has left the meeting.
Gabriel and the others experience a shared terror,
a fear that this young woman is gone for good,
that she will never return,
that she will drink
or pick up a drug.
They are terrified that she will relapse,
that she will die.
Gabriel wants to kill the abusive stranger.
He believes that many sober people in this virtual meeting
want to kill this human being.
Sober people trying to lead principled lives

want to murder another human being.
(Gabriel once heard someone say that the split second
between thought and action
is the grace of God.)
He is grateful that he is not within striking distance
of the abusive stranger.
The split second between thought and action,
he concedes,
is the sublime grace of God.

The Mancunians' apartment is dark.

Neither the man nor the woman is on the terrace

and the rose bushes appear weak and diseased.

(Perhaps the plague has infected the rose bushes too.)

The Mancunians are at the hospital

where the woman is being treated for her illness.

Her husband is not allowed to sit by her side.

He is not allowed to sit in the waiting area.

Instead he waits outside,

on the street,

and clutches a cup of coffee.

His hands shake.

He prays that he will predecease her.

He prays that she will outlive him,

that perhaps she will even find another man

with whom to spend her final years.

He thinks about the long life they have spent together,

how they met when they were children,
how they fell in love,
how they have fought for each other for decades.
He looks to the hospital.
An ambulance pulls into the driveway,
lights and sirens ablaze.
(Death has arrived.)
He pictures his wife in the hospital
with tubes and IVs,
alone and terrified.
He imagines kissing her forehead,
her clammy forehead.
He waves to the hospital,
up to a window on the top floor
where he imagines his wife might be.
I'm right here dear,
he yells.
Right here.
The thought of her alone in the hospital,
attached to machines
and tended to by masked and faceless people,
causes him to drop his coffee to the pavement
and vomit.

In the early evening Gabriel sits at the kitchen table
and eats an egg on toast.
He is unaware of the time or day
and he thinks about the passage of time,
the monolithic devourer of time that has replaced
the measurable linear time that once existed.
The inability to measure time has resulted in
a velocity that terrifies him.
(Nothing is happening
because life moves too fast.
Life moves too fast
because nothing is happening.)
As Gabriel places a plate and glass in the kitchen sink
he hears a sound.
He ignores it and washes the plate.
After a few seconds he hears another sound,
coming from outside,

and then several more.

The clapping of hands.

A wooden spoon against a metal pot.

An air horn.

Tin drums.

Howls and screams.

(Is that a trumpet in the distance?)

What he hears is a symphony of sorts,

a symphony of strange and primitive sounds.

The sounds rise in power and mass

and fuse into one transcendent harmony.

Gabriel looks outside to see what is happening,

what sonic event has descended upon the city.

People hang from their open windows

and stand on roofs.

There across the street is Sophie,

the woman who makes the bed,

blowing on a trumpet.

(Gabriel had projected many qualities on to Sophie

but a mastery of brass instruments

was not one of them.)

The old man directly below her bangs on his copper pot.

The two young doctors also make noise.

The taller man claps his hands.

and his husband roars into a bullhorn.

The socialite holds something aloft.

Is that a kazoo,

Gabriel wonders.

(Yes it is a kazoo.)

Gabriel wonders how the socialite has come to own a kazoo.

He looks down to the Mancunians.

The man from Manchester stands on the terrace,

surrounded by dead rose bushes,

and claps.

With his enormous meaty scarred hands

he claps in appreciation for the professionals

who risk their lives to save others.

He hopes that by clapping

his wife might survive.

(There is of course no cause and effect.)

Gabriel sticks his head out the window

and allows the harmonic breeze to wash over him.

He inhales and breathes in the sounds,

which surround him,

penetrate him.

He reaches for a frying pan and smacks it with a serving spoon.

Bang bang bang.

Gabriel watches Sophie's hopeful face

as she raises her trumpet in victory.

He watches the socialite

and again wonders how she has come to possess a kazoo.

Gabriel experiences something that feels like joy.

(It is not joy

but rather a release,

an eruptive cleansing release.)

He experiences a sense of connection

to the people he has been observing.

Before they were strangers in a diorama,

a tableau vivant,

but now they are something else.

These people,

with their drums and noisemakers,

have become something else.

These people who hang out of windows,

these people who normally would not mix,

these people have somehow become members of one tribe.

(Death has arrived

and as a result people celebrate life.

Gabriel wonders how death sometimes causes people

to celebrate life

and how it sometimes causes people

to curse life,

to curse God.

He cursed God after his daughter died

and he has never stopped.)

Gabriel hangs out the window and howls with rapture.

(It is indeed rapture.)

He feels as if a spirit of some sort has taken hold of his body.

He pounds the frying pan.

He sees the socialite

and she sees him.

She blows the kazoo.

It makes only a low humming sound

and its contribution to the harmonic wave is immaterial.

They wave to each other.

Kazoo,

he screams with joy and affection.

Kazoo,

she yells back,

fucking kazoo!

A procession of ambulances moves up the avenue
shortly after midnight
in a slow yet purposeful advance,
a phalanx of sorts.
For a few seconds the vehicles inadvertently fall into
a tight *V* formation
before devolving back into chaos.
Whether the ambulances carry just the sick,
or also the dead,
is not clear.
Gabriel wonders if they turn off their lights and sirens
when the patient dies en route
or if they keep them on to honor this human being,
to give the dead a final voice,
one last shout to the skies.
The waves of ambulances have not stopped for weeks.
They keep coming,

these rolling tombs.

They are relentless,

inexhaustible.

(And yet they move so slowly.)

They have taken on a character that to Gabriel

appears more menacing

than palliative.

Gabriel recalls the ambulance that arrived twenty-two minutes

after he called for help.

He pictures the EMT who tried to revive his daughter,

how she worked with purpose

and poise

and passion.

He recalls the moment that she looked at her watch,

tapped the watch face

and recorded the time of death.

He recalls the wails that exploded out of his wife's body.

inhuman wails,

cries of the most unspeakable agony.

He can never forget her wails.

They haunt him often.

He will hear them forever.

He recalls the moment that his wife fainted,

how the EMT rushed to her side

and cared for her until she returned.

Gabriel watches another ambulance below.

It is creeping up Amsterdam,

lights and sirens

creating an audio-visual chaos.

Godspeed,

Gabriel whispers.

And then the ambulance

stops at a red light,

with sirens silenced and lights now off.

No,

Gabriel thinks,

no.

The ambulance waits for the light to turn green

and then continues uptown.

The only thing that scares Gabriel more than

an ambulance with sirens blaring

is an ambulance that stops at red lights.

The city has lost its pulse,

its cadence,

its chaos.

So many people have left for the beach

and the suburbs

and the mountains

that Gabriel wonders whether cities will survive the plague.

(He tries to comfort himself with ancient plagues

that failed to extinguish cities.)

The city is quiet,

stripped of cars and trucks,

industry and smokestacks.

Nature has begun to reclaim the city.

(He once saw a documentary that showed Chernobyl

decades after the meltdown.

The irradiated land was overgrown

with trees and plants and flowers.

Birds and deer and mammals of all sorts roamed the dense forests.

Nature wins,

in its way,

if you give it enough time.)

Nature has begun to reclaim this city.

The air is free of smog,

clear and vivid,

vibrant and sweet.

A raft of ducks waddles down West End Avenue.

A fox in Riverside Park disembowels a stray poodle.

A turkey vulture swoops down to tear apart the poodle's carrion.

Grass grows wild

and rises up through pavement cracks.

Creeping ivy slithers up the side of a bus stop.

The city has turned bucolic,

feral.

Gabriel looks out the window.

A bird of prey,

a peregrine falcon,

sits atop the cornice of a nearby building,

scanning the street below for rodents.

The influx of wildlife causes Gabriel to experience

both exhilaration and discomfort.

He wonders which one of these animals,

these insects,

might carry the next wave of death to this city.

A bright green praying mantis,

all legs and wings,

lands on the window ledge.

The mantis clutches a dead cricket in its jaws.

Gabriel winces.

Nature wins.

The two young doctors stand in the nursery
and argue about the pink accent wall.
Gabriel watches them gesticulate wildly
in a manner that suggests they are furious with each other.
The taller of the two men wants to keep the color pink.
He takes the position that pink is a way
to honor their unborn daughter,
to keep her in their hearts.
The shorter of the two men takes the opposite position.
He believes that the pain of the loss is so great
that they need to make the loss
as clear and as definite as possible,
and to do that they will need to paint the pink wall white.
He believes that they require clarity
and a clear delineation
that separates their past loss
from their future.

The affection and healthy compromise

that defined their relationship

has disappeared,

replaced by a hardening of positions

that extends into other areas of their lives.

The proper height for a painting.

Their assessment of their favorite football team's prospects.

The size of their television.

The epidemiology of this plague,

the cause of this plague,

the best way to combat this plague.

Gabriel watches the two men argue

about everything.

He is disheartened

and recalls the arguments with his wife,

each of which chipped at the fragile foundation of their marriage.

He believes that the foundation of every marriage

is fragile,

and that even the slightest damage,

with some repetition,

can cause irreparable harm.

He believes that the margin for error is smaller

than most realize.

(Several married couples were irritated by his belief

in the fragility of marriage

and called him cynical.

Two of those couples subsequently divorced.)

The shorter of the two men,

the emergency room doctor,

storms out of the nursery

and slams the door behind him.

The taller of the two,

the anesthesiologist,

sits down on the floor of the nursery

and looks around,

at the disassembled changing table,

at the mobile that hangs from the ceiling,

at the box that contains the crib,

at the pink accent wall.

The man stands up

and screams

and screams

and screams

and punches a hole

in the pink accent wall.

The other man hears his screams

and hears the punch to the wall

but does not move to comfort his husband.

He stays in the other room,

separate now,

disconnected.

The Mancunian stands on the sidewalk
and looks up to the hospital.
He searches for some sign of his wife,
for some sign that she is recovering,
that she lives.
The ambulances are lined up in front of the entrance
to the emergency room,
idling with lights on and sirens off.
They unload their precious cargo,
some barely living
and some dead.
The man finishes his coffee and sits down at a nearby bench.
The nurse said that he would come outside,
two hours ago,
and give the Mancunian an update.
The man waits impatiently for news of his wife's condition.
As he sits on the bench he begins to replay

the reel of their lives together.
He starts in grade school when they were just children.
He pictures the girl who was chatty and popular
when he was withdrawn and invisible.
He pictures their first kiss,
in a movie theater,
in the middle of Swiss Family Robinson.
The Mancunian rolls the reel forward,
to their wedding day,
to the enormous wedding band on his left ring finger
that cost an extra ten quid because of the size.
He recalls the shame he felt at the additional expense,
at the burden he felt he had brought to his wife.
The memories become too painful for the Mancunian
and he shuts them off.
A doctor walks out of the hospital and looks around.
She sees the Mancunian on the bench
and walks toward the man
who is waiting for news about his wife.
The man rises from the bench and stands at attention.
(He once served in the military
and sixty years later
he still stands at attention

when deference is implied.)
The doctor's head is down.
She looks exhausted,
pale,
drained,
defeated.
She trembles as she tells the Mancunian,
I'm so sorry but your wife has died.
The man knew that his wife would die.
His wife too knew that she would die.
(Her last thoughts before she took her final breath were,
Who is going to look after
my dear Patrick?)
She's in the morgue now,
the doctor says,
and you can go see her if you'd like.
But only for five minutes,
the new rules since all this.
The exhausted and pale and drained and defeated doctor turns
and walks back to the hospital.
(She has delivered this news hundreds of times
over the past several months.)
The Mancunian watches the doctor walk away.

He admires the professionals who took care of his wife,

who tried to save her.

He is grateful for their service,

that they have risked death to fulfill their oath.

He admires all of those who fulfill honorable oaths.

He has no time for those who fulfill dishonorable oaths.

(An oath is neither a weapon nor a shield,

he often said.)

The Mancunian is terrified.

He is terrified to be alone for the first time in seventy years.

He is terrified of loneliness,

of facing the final days of his life without her.

He decides not to see his wife in the morgue.

He does not want to see her body.

He does not want to add that image to the reel of the beautiful life

that they spent together.

He starts to walk home

but he has forgotten where he lives.

He takes out his wallet

and looks at the card that his wife made for him.

On the card is written his name and address.

Alone he walks north,

up Tenth Avenue,

toward their home,

toward what is now his home.

On his way there he decides to join his wife.

He decides to join his wife soon.

He decides that he must protect her in the afterlife.

He imagines their reunion.

Together they will prune rosebushes

and listen to The Hollies

and The Dakotas

and Herman's Hermits.

The Mancunian walks for fifteen minutes

and realizes that again he has forgotten where he lives.

He reaches for his wallet,

for the card his wife had inserted,

and he is overcome with panic and confusion,

for he realizes that

his wallet is gone,

lost.

He continues walking in the direction that he believes

might take him home.

He hopes that he will see something that will jog his memory,

perhaps a restaurant or a store or a street sign.

He walks for fifteen minutes

but sees nothing.

Disoriented,

he sits down on the sidewalk,

on the ground,

in front of the subway station.

I'm done,

he thinks.

People pass him but do not look at him.

(He exists

but he does not exist.)

The Mancunian looks for his wife among the passersby.

(She is in the morgue.)

Gabriel approaches the plaza in front of the subway station.

He is on his way home from the market.

His head is lowered

and he pays little attention to the few people on the street.

As he passes the subway entrance he glances over

and sees the Mancunian

sitting on the pavement

with his mask pulled down over his chin.

He is alarmed to see the man sitting on the ground.

Gabriel stops and approaches the man.

Do you need help,

he asks.

The man looks up.

My wife is dead and I forgot where I live,

forgot my name too.

Gabriel thinks about the many times he watched

this man and his wife

prune the rose bushes.

I know where you live,

he says.

I can take you there.

Gabriel extends his hand.

The Mancunian reaches up and grabs it.

Gabriel is taken by the size and strength of the man's hand.

He helps lift the man up

and they proceed uptown,

in silence.

Gabriel leads the Mancunian to the front door of his building,

and it is only at this moment,

when the man sees his and his wife's last name

on the building directory,

that he recalls who he is

and where he lives.

The socialite has received an invitation
to a virtual event
celebrating the publication of a noted author's new book.
She has received several invitations in recent weeks
but has declined each one because of her distaste for all things virtual.
(It is the energy of personal contact that acts
as a balm for her sadness,
and it is the inert energy of virtual contact that acts
as an accelerant to her sadness.)
Despite her apprehension she decides to attend
this virtual literary event.
She is desperate for some sort of connection.
Gabriel looks over to the apartment of the socialite.
He watches as she sits at her vanity and applies makeup
in anticipation of this virtual gathering.
The woman puckers her lips.

She pats a blotter to her forehead.
She admires herself in the mirror
and then takes a deep gulp of wine.
She opens her computer and logs on to the gathering.
There on the screen are many people she knows.
A patron of a museum.
A scion of wealthy industrialists.
A female hedge fund manager.
Two novelists,
one painter
and a gallery owner.
The socialite smiles and waves to the other people.
Some wave in return
but some do not see her and stare blankly at the screen.
The host,
an English woman who claims some dubious royal lineage,
asks the attendees to raise their glasses
and toast the celebrated author.
The attendees,
the socialite included,
comply and raise their glasses.
The host says a few laudatory words about the author
and then makes a motion indicating the tapping of glasses.

The socialite leans her glass toward the screen

and joins others who also lean their glasses forward.

She takes a sip of wine.

The toast is unsatisfying to the socialite

as it lacks the clinking sound of glass on glass

that she so loves.

The celebrated author discusses his latest book.

He talks pompously about the creative process

and his daily writing routine,

which consists of great discipline

and organic food

and several liters of alkaline water

and deep breathing exercises.

The author finishes his discussion

and opens up the event for questions.

The first question is from a man who asks,

What does it take to be a writer?

What does it *really* take to be a writer?

Before the author can answer,

the screen freezes.

(Thank God,

as there is nothing more tiresome

than listening to a writer talk about

what it takes to be a writer.)

The movement of each attendee stops,

offering only a blurry image of the person

trapped in their home.

The socialite taps the screen.

When that does not release the attendees from their frozen state

she taps a few keys on the keyboard.

This too does nothing.

She logs off of the virtual event

and tries to dial back in,

but is unable to do so.

A message on the screen indicates that the event has been cancelled

because of technical difficulties.

The socialite stares at the blank screen on her laptop.

She gently taps the screen as if to determine if it is dead or alive.

(The party is over.)

She closes the screen and looks around her empty room.

There are no caterers cleaning up after an evening of revelry.

There are no musicians putting away their instruments.

There is no evidence of people having

come together.

She is once again left alone with her thoughts.

She is afflicted with feelings of insecurity,

of not being loved.

(She never knew her father.)

There are times when she is convinced that she is vapid

and stupid

and lacking substance.

(In fact she is none of these things.

She is smart

and thoughtful

and generous.)

Without the parties

and the people

and the activity

there is nothing to distract her

from unbearable feelings of solitude.

She is incapable of being alone for extended periods of time.

The socialite glances at the bottle of pills on the vanity.

She thinks about the prospects of a life without festivity.

She cannot bear a life without festivity.

With her back to the window

she pours all of the pills into her palm.

There are twenty-nine benzodiazepines in total.

She swallows the pills

and finishes off the bottle of wine.

She lowers the blinds

and lays down on the bed.

She turns on the television,

a comedy,

and listens to the noise

and the laugh track,

and she watches the actors move about the screen.

The noise and the laugh track and the movement give her comfort

in these final moments

of her life.

The old man walks in a hurry around his apartment.
As usual he wears a shirt and boxer shorts and socks.
The television is on in the background.
(The governor is updating people on the dire state of things.)
The man stops at the kitchen table
and lifts the dented copper pot to his lips,
consuming the remaining drops of cauliflower soup.
He notices on the floor a fragment from the porcelain angel
that he broke earlier.
He picks it up,
examines it with regret
and throws it in the trash.
He remains consumed with guilt over having broken
the porcelain angel.
Gabriel watches as the man fills a valise with clothing
and toiletries
and a photograph of his wife.

(Gabriel wonders where this man could be going.)

The old man puts on a collared shirt

and a sweater,

pants and shoes.

He sits on the sofa with his packed bag by his feet.

He rests his palms on his upper legs

and sits with his back erect.

He waits on the sofa for several hours

with his bag by his feet.

He waits for his daughter to pick him up and bring him Upstate,

to the country,

where there are fewer people,

where they are spread out,

where the air is fresh,

where it safer than the city.

Where people can survive.

As light turns to dark

the man stands up.

He looks down at himself,

at his sweater

and his collared shirt

and pants

and shoes.

Foolish me,
he thinks.
He walks to the kitchen
and makes himself
a bowl of pasta.

Sophie is again sick,

fatigued,

short of breath.

Her initial recovery was short-lived.

She has lost her taste for food

and her appetite is depressed.

Her fever has lifted though

and she feels marginally better.

She believes that the worst is behind her.

She is optimistic by nature.

Despite her many disappointments

she remains optimistic.

Gabriel no longer hides behind the drapes

when looking across the street

to the woman who makes the bed.

Sophie in turn takes some comfort in the developing familiarity

between the two.

When making the bed she might glance in Gabriel's direction
to see if he is in his apartment.
Sometimes she sees no movement there,
just a dark and still space.
Sometimes she sees Gabriel moving about,
making coffee,
cleaning,
exercising,
pacing.
(He paces frequently
and with great exertion.
He walks as if he is angry with the floor.)
Sometimes she sees him in the frame of a window
as he watches the world around him
and the Mancunians
and the two young doctors
and the old man
and the socialite
and Sophie herself.
She takes comfort in watching him,
for she has corrected the asymmetry
that once existed between them.
Gabriel too is comforted by this new symmetry,

relieved by it.

He no longer feels intrusive and inappropriate.

Sophie holds a cup of hot tea in both hands

and looks out her window.

Gabriel holds a cup of hot coffee in both hands

and looks out his window.

Sophie waves to Gabriel.

Gabriel waves to Sophie.

He makes a motion with his hand that suggests

stay right there,

be back in a minute.

She nods and raises her right thumb.

Gabriel runs to his closet and removes an old white sheet.

He cuts it in half with scissors,

takes out a marker and writes the words

Are you okay?

He runs back to the window

and sees Sophie across the way.

She stands in the frame of her window,

awaiting his return.

Gabriel holds the sheet up to the window.

Are you okay?

Sophie disappears for a moment

and comes back with glasses on.

She reads his message.

She again raises her right thumb.

She points in his direction

as if to ask him the same question.

(Are you okay?)

He raises his right thumb in affirmation.

(Yes I am okay.)

She smiles and waves goodbye.

With blinds open she gets back under the covers of her bed

and takes a nap.

Gabriel turns away.

He does not watch Sophie sleep.

He wants to maintain symmetry,

to avoid the asymmetry of the past.

The Mexican restaurant is closed,

shuttered,

insolvent.

Gabriel is outside for his daily thirty-minute walk.

On his way to the park

he stops in front of the empty restaurant.

He views his reflection in the window.

(He wears two masks on his face

and a pair of surgical gloves.)

He looks inside the restaurant.

He recalls Rosa and the personal information

that she shared with him.

(She crossed the border at great risk.

A coyote put a cigarette out on her arm.

She enjoys taking her family to minor league baseball games.)

He thinks about the fleeting connections he has made in his life

and how the pain of their endings is often disproportionate

to the length and substance of those relationships.
He concludes that the end of a short and superficial relationship,
a minor loss,
can indeed cause feelings
of tremendous loss.
He has come to understand that
these feelings of loss may have little to do
with the particular person or relationship,
but rather may be the result of some historical wound,
specific or uncertain,
known or unknown,
that is accessed and relived through the minor loss.
He worries about Rosa.
He fears that her husband,
the nurse,
is at great risk of the contagion
and that by extension Rosa and her family
may be at great risk too.
Gabriel scans the restaurant.
He sees on the floor a pile of discarded clothing and papers.
There in the pile is the apron that Rosa once wore,
her name stitched on the front pocket.
The pile begins to move

and he takes a step back in fear,

even though he is outside and the movement is inside.

Given the state of the shuttered restaurant

he suspects that what moves beneath the trash is a rat.

There is more movement

and from underneath Rosa's apron

emerges not a rat,

but a beautiful cat,

a silver Abyssinian.

The cat takes a quick and skeptical glance at Gabriel

and then glides away,

across the dusty floor.

Gabriel watches as the sleek cat,

now master of this abandoned domain,

jumps up on the counter and drinks from a dripping faucet.

A police officer walks his beat along Amsterdam.

With his surgical mask

and his dark sunglasses

and his eight-point hat pulled down low,

the officer appears not to have a face.

With some trepidation

Gabriel greets the officer

and points to the stray cat in the restaurant.

The officer stares at the cat,

which in turn watches the two men

on the other side of the glass.

The cat jumps down from the counter

and glides across the floor

and burrows back under the pile of clothing,

beneath Rosa's apron.

The cop shrugs his shoulders

and continues his walk uptown.

Gabriel looks at the pile of clothing

and then at the departing officer,

who disappears around the corner.

Both the cat and the cop are gone.

Gabriel fears that he is seeing ghosts.

Again.

The old man sleeps on his sofa.

He is fully clothed

and his packed valise stands on the floor nearby.

His daughter did not pick him up

as she said she would.

He is disappointed

but not surprised.

He does not know why she treats him with such indifference.

(Some might say that she treats him with cruelty.)

He once asked her why she treats him

with such indifference.

She smiled and said,

I don't know what you're talking about Dad,

I love you

and you know that.

He has tried to accept that her indifference

may have nothing to do with him,

that she simply might be the type of person who expresses love
in untraditional ways.
(She does not express love in the way
many express their love.)
The man awakens.
He looks around the room,
surprised that he has fallen asleep on the sofa,
in his clothes,
with his valise nearby.
He looks at his watch and sees that it is early morning.
A siren roars outside
and then another
and another.
They move in sequence,
separated by no more than a few seconds.
Two ambulances move side by side,
their sirens layered on top of each other
so that they create one steady stream
of the most painful and piercing sound.
(Death is busy this morning,
he thinks.)
He wonders if he will survive in this city.
He looks up to the ceiling and wonders about the noise

he had heard from above,

if the person who lives there is okay.

(Sophie has been recovering slowly.)

He moves to the kitchen and makes himself a cup of cereal.

He stands near the window and looks down to the ambulances.

Every few seconds he eats a spoonful of cereal.

He wonders what his daughter's life is like Upstate.

She has lived there for five years

but he has never seen her home.

She has never invited him to see her home.

He shrugs his shoulders as if to accept the reality of his life,

a surrender to things that will forever remain out of his influence.

The man is startled by a sound that is at first unfamiliar to him.

It is a sound that he has heard in the past,

but so infrequently that he cannot identify it.

He hears the sound again

and recognizes it

as his doorbell.

He has so few visitors that

he hears the sound of his doorbell

only two or three times per year.

He moves to the door and peers through the peephole.

(Given the state of things

he cannot open the door without assessing

the risk of the encounter.

He cannot be close to strangers.

Strangers equal death.)

He is at first confused by what he sees,

by whom he sees.

He closes his eyes and leans his forehead against the door.

Tears form in his eyes

and he shakes his head in disbelief.

He opens the door

and takes one step back.

His daughter stands before him.

He does not move toward her because he fears rejection.

She steps through the doorway

and into the apartment.

She hugs him

and he hugs her back.

(How long he has waited for her to express her love

in traditional ways.)

The woman looks around and points to the valise.

She lifts the bag and carries it out to the car.

She gets him settled in the passenger's seat.

The car is cold and she puts a blanket over him.

She hands him a fried egg sandwich and a cup of coffee.

You're going to like it Upstate,

she says.

Gabriel thinks about the people he has been observing
and the stories
he has constructed
and the attributes
he has assigned to these strangers.
There is Sophie.
The socialite.
The old man with the copper pot.
The two young doctors.
The two Mancunians.
(Two of these people have died,
one has moved Upstate
and four remain.)
Gabriel glances over to the apartment of the two young doctors.
For days he has not seen any activity in their home,
but he now sees that they have returned from their jobs.
They have been working at the hospital

for seventy-two straight hours,
with only a few short naps and even fewer meals.
Many of their patients have died.
(Each death is a form of ambiguous loss,
for they do not know the people who have died.)
Tonight they enter the apartment quietly.
They drop their clothes on the floor
and put them in the washing machine.
They shower and put on fresh clothes,
one after the next.
One eats pizza at the table
and the other eats pizza in front of the television.
When they cross paths in the kitchen
the taller doctor says something cutting and cruel to his husband,
who in turn replies with a vicious barb
about the other man's family,
a barb that cuts to the heart of his deepest fears and vulnerabilities.
(The taller man's parents hate their son
and refuse to acknowledge the marriage between
these two men.
The shorter man's parents adore their son
and celebrate the marriage between
these two men.

The difference in the families' reactions
has been the source of great pain
for both of these men.)
Unlike the happier times from just weeks ago
they have become so irritated with each other
that they now sleep in separate rooms.
The taller of the two sleeps in the bedroom
and the shorter one sleeps on the couch in the living room.
The laughter and camaraderie that once defined their relationship
has disappeared,
replaced by a chilly distance.
The stress of their work
under the most difficult and terrifying conditions,
combined with the trauma of losing their unborn child,
has caused significant damage to their relationship.
Gabriel has himself experienced
the agonizing and chilly distance that replaces
laughter and camaraderie.
He has experienced the futility of reversing course,
of reestablishing a connection to someone
who was once so close
but who is now so far away.
Gabriel recalls those brutal months

following their daughter's death,

how he and his wife tried to find

even a few seconds of joy in a day,

how they tried to make love

but could only cry in bed

with their backs turned to each other.

Gabriel has come to believe that the greatest distance in life,

the most insurmountable chasm,

is those three inches

between the backs

of two people

who were once

in love.

Gabriel wonders how the Mancunian is doing
now that his wife has died.
He wonders what has become of their
Welsh springer spaniel.
He looks down to the terrace
and sees that the man is pruning the rose bushes.
Without his wife though
he has created a catastrophe of sorts.
He has massacred the bushes
and cut them down to their stalks.
Flowers and branches cover the terrace floor.
The man has lost control of the garden hose
and he has flooded the area with water and mud.
He appears to have been so careless with the shears that his hands
are covered in cuts and blood.
Gabriel is concerned by the man's cognitive decline
and dangerous behavior.

In the past the man's wife was there to care for him,
to enforce the boundaries that his mind could no longer set,
but in her absence his disordered mind,
exacerbated by the magnitude of her loss,
has taken him to a place of the most chaotic despair.
(Gabriel has been in a similar place,
when his loss and his depression
conspired to take him to a place of the most chaotic despair.)
Gabriel fears for the man's well-being.
He wonders if he should call emergency
and have an ambulance come for the man.
He thinks about all of those who have died
when they have been taken to the hospital.
He thinks about the odds of the man surviving the hospital
versus the odds of the man surviving at home,
alone.
(The odds of both are quite low.)
Gabriel considers the man's bloody hands.
He calls emergency and provides the address of the Mancunian.
He watches the street below,
looking for the ambulance.
The ambulance arrives in four minutes.
(Gabriel wonders if his daughter might have survived

if the ambulance had arrived in

four minutes.)

He watches the EMTs enter the building

and then watches as they speak with the Mancunian.

The man offers his two hands,

wrists turned upward as if he is being arrested.

(He was arrested several times in Manchester when he was young.

He turned his life around when his wife gave him an ultimatum.)

The EMT gently guides his hands downward

to indicate that he is not being arrested,

to indicate that he is safe.

The EMT leads him out of the apartment,

out of the building

and into the ambulance.

Gabriel prays that he has made the right decision.

He experiences the unbearable weight of having made

a life or death decision for another human being,

and of having done so without their knowledge or consent.

As the ambulance turns up Amsterdam,

sirens and lights ablaze,

Gabriel hears a sound.

And then another

and another.

Seven o'clock has arrived.
He runs into the kitchen
and grabs a pot and a wood serving spoon.
He hangs out the window and taps the pot.
He thinks about the Mancunian,
about the decision he made to call the ambulance.
(Gabriel does not see the Mancunian again
and does not know if the man has died
or survived and moved elsewhere,
perhaps back to England.
The Mancunian in fact goes into cardiac arrest
in the ambulance that Gabriel called
and dies before he reaches the hospital.
Gabriel does not know that the man has died in the ambulance,
that there may be a causal relationship
between Gabriel's actions
and the Mancunian's death.
Gabriel and his former wife
are tormented by any causal relationship between action,
or inaction,
and death.)
He pounds the pot.
He pounds it again with unbridled force.

He looks across the street

and there is Sophie.

She hangs out the window

and plays her trumpet.

She holds the trumpet aloft

and howls to Gabriel.

He howls back in delight.

The depopulated city is alive with a harmony

of fury and faith,

an orchestra

of the living.

The two young doctors have just returned
from a forty-eight-hour shift at the hospital,
and after this gruesome experience they do not want to speak.
What they have seen is too difficult to describe,
to discuss,
to relive.
What they desire now is mindless entertainment.
They sit on opposite ends of the couch
and watch the baseball game.
(Gabriel watches the same game,
but five seconds after the doctors.)
Between innings one man reaches for the other's hand.
This touching of hands is the first physical contact
they have had in weeks.
With some reluctance,
and some relief,
the other man reciprocates.

The shorter of the two is an optimist and he notes that
although the gap between them is not closing,
it is not growing either.
The taller of the two is less optimistic and he counters that
although the gap between them is not growing,
it is not closing either.
The two men laugh.
(Since they met in medical school
they have laughed about their different views of life.
One is always more hopeful than the other.)
They move closer to each other,
to the center of the sofa.
They again hold hands
and when a batter on their favorite teams hits a homerun
they jump up
and yell
and hug each other.
This moment of spontaneous affection and joy surprises them.
They have become unaccustomed to moments like this.
They register their surprise
and then with great affection
hug again.

In the city
there is a marginal reopening,
a sliver of hope.
The microbe at last struggles to find suitable hosts,
to find cellular crevices in which to hide and replenish,
to locate havens from which to launch fresh attacks.
After many millions of tiny steps
immunity of the herd has begun to take hold,
and after what seems like one great step
but is really the last of several million great steps,
science has begun to prevail.
The most minimal public activity returns to the city.
People no longer leave their homes only for food
or for thirty minutes of exercise.
People are now permitted to walk the streets for pleasure,
for recreation
or for no reason at all.

Still masked,

still anonymous to their fellow city dwellers,

they revel in a freedom long forgotten.

They wander around as if they are strangers in a strange land.

They point in awe to shops now closed,

out of business,

and to dormant churches,

thick chains securing the holy doors,

and to empty playgrounds

where gusts of wind carry trash in wild and violent circles.

They point to overgrown grass

and trees

and ivy.

They point to a wildness of nature.

People gawk as if they have discovered an ancient land,

a lost civilization of sorts.

They act as if they have returned to a place they once knew

but that now only strikes a thin chord of familiarity.

These people know they are home,

they can feel it,

but with each traversed city block

they learn anew,

as if they have arrived after being abroad for many years.

Gabriel walks the streets.
He too learns anew.
He looks at the eyes of others.
He looks for people he knows,
perhaps people from his meetings,
or Sophie,
or friends of his deceased daughter.
(Although so many years have passed,
they are still uncomfortable when they see Gabriel.
They do not know what to say
or how to act.)
He feels as though he is walking a city
that existed long before he moved here,
before prosperity arrived.
A primordial city.
He experiences a sense of temporal dislocation
which causes him to think about the non-linearity of time
that the plague has created,
how the monolithic devourer of time has replaced
the measurable linearity of time that once existed,
and how the present has somehow become
the distant past.
A woman approaches him.

Because she wears a mask and a hat,

only a thin strip of flesh and eyes are visible.

He thinks he recognizes this woman from

her gait and her eyes.

(She is not Sophie.)

He nods to her

and she nods back

and they keep walking in opposite directions.

He finds this exchange to be unsatisfying.

He has connected

but he has not connected.

He thinks he knows her

but he does not know if he knows her.

Gabriel approaches the intersection and sees two parked cars,

each decades old,

from the Fifties or Sixties.

He is reminded of the old cars in Cuba

that also have the effect

of warping time,

of causing time to fall back upon itself.

Gabriel feels as though he is suffocating,

as though the distortion of time

is suffocating him.

He wants to tether himself

to a point in time,

to a specific point in time.

He turns and runs home.

He steps into his bedroom.

He lies down on the bed

and holds the baby blanket to his chest.

He is soon soothed.

Gabriel is transported to the past,

to a glorious moment,

which prompts in him

the most pleasing ache.

Gabriel has a guilty pleasure,

an online tabloid from the United Kingdom

that publishes the most scandalous things

about the most famous people.

In his work he attempts to bring beauty

to mundane household objects.

(His iconic corkscrew

and his award-winning axe.)

His reading of this tabloid stands in opposition

to the beauty he seeks through his work.

While he hopes that his well-designed objects

might somehow elevate those who use them,

he concedes that the tabloid accomplishes the opposite.

The tabloid for him represents

all that is base

and vulgar

and pornographic

and judgmental

and petty

and superficial

and tawdry.

He wonders if his affinity for this tabloid

comes from the same faulty wiring that led him,

at different times in his life,

to be addicted to alcohol

and drugs

and irresponsible sex

and sarcasm

and resentment

and self-pity

and spending

and sugar

and caffeine

and nicotine

and asymmetry

and stock market speculation

and contemporary French ceramics.

(He believes that the same wiring is the cause.)

Gabriel enjoys his breakfast while he reads the tabloid.

He is alarmed to see that the famous performer,

the young woman who was cruelly disparaged
in the virtual meeting,
has relapsed.
The tabloid carries a photograph of her in a state of disarray,
slumped behind the wheel of a parked car
with a glass pipe pressed to her lips.
The tabloid has published numerous photographs of her,
including one where tears run down her cheeks
and one where she pleads
for the paparazzo to stop.
Gabriel becomes enraged.
He is revolted by what he is reading.
He feels sickened by the asymmetry that exists
when millions of people watch a person in distress.
He thinks with regret about the dynamic that once existed
when he watched Sophie make the bed,
before she restored symmetry
by watching him in return.
He turns off the computer
and vows never again to read this tabloid
or to engage in other forms of asymmetry.
(He never again reads this tabloid.)
He is incapable of enjoying anything in moderation.

He either indulges to excess or abstains entirely.

He has so far excised entirely from his life

alcohol

and drugs

and irresponsible sex

and sarcasm

and spending

and nicotine

and asymmetry

and stock market speculation.

Although he has tried

he has not been able to excise

resentment

or self-pity

or sugar

or caffeine

or contemporary French ceramics.

In the evening Gabriel dials in to the virtual meeting.

As the square tiles fill up with familiar faces

he hopes to see the face of the famous young performer

who was exploited by the tabloid

in a revolting act of intrusion.

The meeting begins

but the performer does not join.

The old-timers,

the protective women who have been coming to these meetings

for decades,

ask if anyone has spoken with the young woman.

(No one has spoken with the young woman.)

They have called her and texted her

but she has not replied.

These protective women,

these women who have been leading sober

and responsible

and principled

lives for many years,

now express a primal desire to murder the man

who said cruel and disparaging things about the young woman.

(They express this desire

because they feel it intensely

and because to not express it might lead to relapse.

They say it to save their own lives.)

Several other members of the group express similar desires.

There is laughter when an octogenarian

who is confined to a wheelchair

says he too wants to kill.

An old gangster from Hell's Kitchen also articulates
a desire to kill.
No one laughs because they understand
the character and the past of this man.
(These sober and sometimes principled people
take pride in knowing that a member of their clan
is capable of extreme violence.)
In this particular meeting
there is no healing.
There is only rage.

Gabriel looks over to Sophie

and sees that she is preparing her apartment for a visitor.

He is relieved,

even happy,

because her preparation indicates that she has recovered

from her illness.

His joy dissipates

when he sees that Sophie

dims the lights

and lights candles

and straightens the throw pillows on the sofa

and rearranges flowers in the vase

and examines her face in the mirror.

From past experience he knows that these preparations

often indicate that a man will come over.

Gabriel is surprised by the emotions that arise in him.

Self-pity and resentment build.

Jealousy boils.

He knows that he has no right to feel

self-pity or resentment or jealousy.

He also believes that the lack of justification

is a conditional element of jealousy.

As he watches her prepare

he wonders if an asymmetry has crept back into their interaction.

(Yes it has.)

When Sophie walks to the window,

without so much as a glance in his direction,

and lowers the blinds,

he understands that symmetry has been restored.

Gabriel experiences a nausea

that ascends to despair.

(Given his limited interaction with Sophie,

he has suffered a loss

so minor and so ambiguous

that he would be ashamed

to describe it to another human being.)

Gabriel watches the lowered blinds for a few minutes

and then turns away.

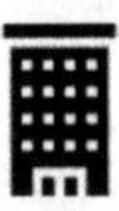

The city's minor rebirth has inspired in Gabriel a desire
to get back to work,
to create new and elegant industrial designs.
(Since death descended upon the city,
he has been uninspired,
uncreative,
unproductive.
He has only the shortest attention span.
He cannot even read a book,
instead spending most of his time watching television
and observing people in nearby buildings
and speculating about their lives.)
He sits at his desk
and considers the products that he might design.
Gabriel has a shoebox that contains
many of his most cherished mementos.
In the shoebox he keeps

commemorative coins that mark each anniversary of his sobriety
and his daughter's first baby tooth
and the rose petals that were placed on his grandmother's body
after she died
and a Tom Seaver rookie baseball card that his father gave him
and three expired passports
and the wedding ring that his former wife insisted on returning
to him when she left
and a fragment of masonry from the jail
where he spent three days after a drunken fight
and a piece of bark from his childhood tree house
and the bracelet that his daughter wore when she passed.
The commemorative coins and the baseball card represent
happiness or success.
The expired passports record the linear velocity of time
that once existed,
before the plague.
Everything else invokes in him either melancholy or shame.
Gabriel believes that people often store
their most important mementos
in shoeboxes.
He also believes that shoeboxes lack the requisite craftsmanship
and fail to capture the importance of the items within.

He thus resolves to create a more beautiful and respectful vessel
for these important objects.
He spends several hours sketching different designs.
Inspired by his love of contemporary French ceramics
he settles upon a design
that is intended to be organic
and shapely
and sinuous
and earthy
and serious
and which possesses a substantial heft.
He draws small compartments in the vessel to hold each memento.
Gabriel holds up the paper and considers his design.
After a few moments of consideration
he concludes that this work falls well short
of his famous corkscrew and his award-winning axe.
His addiction to self-pity returns for a few seconds.
He is ashamed and decides to negate these indulgent feelings
with the more potent and superseding addictions
of caffeine and sugar.
On his way to the kitchen to make
a double cappuccino
with two cubes of raw sugar

and chocolate powder on top,
he eyes not Sophie's drawn blinds
but instead the two young doctors who,
to Gabriel's amazement,
reassemble the changing table and crib
in the spare room,
in what was once the nursery.
They attach the mobile to the ceiling
and set a diaper bin in the corner.
Gabriel considers the possibility that these men
are reliving their trauma
in ways that he himself
often relives his traumas.
(By commemorating a loss.)
Have they gone mad,
he wonders.
Have they gone mad,
just like me.

Gabriel has attended many hundreds of meetings
in dozens of church basements since he hit bottom,
when he looked in the mirror
and saw a man he did not recognize
and a weariness of the soul that foretold oblivion.
He steps into the room
and sees the people he has not seen in person for a long time.
With the exuberance that often comes
from an overdue family reunion,
he greets the famous retired athlete
and the firefighter
and the two cops
and the politician who resigned in disgrace
and the prostitute
and the high school teacher
and the doorman
and the college professor

and the Orthodox rabbi

and the bank robber

and the bank president

and the man from Hell's Kitchen who is comfortable with violence.

There is a celebratory mood in the room.

There is much hugging

and back-slapping

and hand-shaking

and fist-bumping

and air-kissing.

In the corner,

though,

huddled around a table,

are the elderly women who protect the young women.

Gabriel notices that these protectors are crying,

that they comfort each other.

He wonders about the cause of their grief.

He is concerned

and approaches one of the women when she stands to get coffee.

He asks why the women are crying,

what has happened.

The woman reaches for Gabriel's elbow.

The girl,

she says through tears,

that lovely young girl,

the one who tried so hard,

she's gone you know,

gone.

Gone,

he asks in disbelief,

and the woman nods.

Drugs,

she says.

Gabriel's legs shake.

He grieves the death of this young woman,

the famous performer

who was attacked without mercy at the virtual meeting,

who was photographed holding a glass pipe by a paparazzo.

He recalls the brutal asymmetry that exposed her to the world

at her most vulnerable moment.

He becomes overcome with a grief so vast

that he struggles to stand,

to breathe.

He hyperventilates.

His palms sweat.

(He once spoke with a psychotherapist who told him that

if it's hysterical,

it's historical.

He was annoyed by the therapist's pithy little sayings,

cutesy adages passed off as rich oral history.)

Gabriel mourns the death of the young woman,

but he also mourns for his daughter.

Unable to manage his emotions

Gabriel flees the room before the meeting starts.

He fears that the group's grief and rage

will be too painful for him to endure.

He returns home.

He stands in the dark

and glances in the direction of

the Mancunians' vacant apartment

and the old man's vacant apartment

and the socialite's vacant apartment

and the vacant Mexican restaurant

and the young doctors' apartment

and the lowered blinds that conceal

the apartment of the woman who makes the bed.

Sophie.

He fears that she no longer represents

Possibility.

The city,

and life in general,

reopens in small increments.

Each day more people walk the streets and parks.

Fewer masks are worn

and Gabriel finds himself enjoying the parade of faces.

He looks into peoples' eyes.

(Sometimes they look back.)

He smiles at those with kind faces.

(Sometimes they smile back.)

He nods in the direction of parents guiding their energetic children

through the increasingly congested streets.

(They never nod back.)

People move about with the excitement of the newly emancipated.

Something has happened that at first Gabriel does not recognize

but soon becomes apparent to him.

After strolling around for a few hours

he realizes that all is not well on the streets.
Where people once walked on the right side of the sidewalk,
mimicking the flow of traffic,
they now walk on both sides,
weaving sometimes from right to left
and back again.
There is thus frequent physical contact between strangers,
the glancing of shoulders
and knuckles
and bags.
Despite the fear of pestilence
people no longer observe the physical space of others.
The social compact appears to have broken down.
Gabriel fears that the social compact will further erode,
that people will have
less and less regard
for the rights of others.
A pedestrian swings her bag into Gabriel's knee
and walks away without apology.
Gabriel rues the loss of civility,
the most ambiguous of losses.

The two doctors stare at the pink accent wall.

They shake their heads

and laugh

and wonder how they had conformed

to such traditional gender roles.

The taller of the two men,

whose parents do not accept his sexuality

or his husband,

tells a painful story from his childhood

about the colors blue and pink.

His husband gives him a hug.

With rollers and brushes the men paint the wall a neutral tan.

One man taps the mobile and watches it spin.

I'll think she'll love it here,

he says.

(The surrogate has gotten pregnant again.

She and the baby are healthy

and the due date is in three weeks.)
Gabriel watches with such excitement
that he stands up on a chair
to get a better look at the nursery.
He thinks about the excitement they will feel
when they first bring the baby home,
the first feedings,
the first diaper changes,
the first fears and terrors.
(He thinks about the early weeks of his own daughter's life,
when he feared that an osprey might snatch her
as she lay on the beach in Shelter Island.
His wife laughed at him and said,
That's impossible.
He agreed but thought there was a slim possibility
that an osprey could do such a thing.)
Gabriel turns to Sophie's apartment
and sees that the blinds are still lowered.
Weeks have now passed
and the blinds have remained lowered.
He knows that she is still alive,
that she still lives there,
because the lights go on and off throughout the day and night,

and because the bathroom window fogs up with steam
when she takes a shower.
He cannot see her though.
He has come to accept that whatever fleeting connection
once existed between them
is nothing more than a fleeting
and immaterial interaction.
He has come to accept that he has projected
many qualities and traits
onto the woman who makes the bed.
He has come to believe that her name is Sophie.
She is smart.
She is funny.
She is compassionate.
She is tortured.
She has beautiful penmanship.
She is restless.
She is brave.
She enjoys tart fruits.
She was orphaned at a young age.
She has a large and loving family.
She is not a smoker but sneaks an occasional cigarette.
She is principled.

She is prone to bouts of melancholy.
She is creative.
She enjoys Nineteenth Century Russian literature.
She makes a delicious savory pie.
For Gabriel the woman across the way once represented
Possibility.
(As he has let go of magical thinking,
the woman no longer represents
Possibility.)
For a few months,
amidst the contagion's wrath,
amidst the resulting isolation,
he had fantasized that this woman could save him.
(He knows that no woman can save him.
He knows that no person or thing
can save him.)
Gabriel watches the lights dance behind Sophie's blinds.
Something catches his eye
and he looks closer.
Someone has raised the blinds,
just a few inches.
He wonders if Sophie has raised the blinds
or if someone else has done so.

A sliver of light peeks out from her apartment,

four inches of light.

Gabriel cannot see inside.

All he can see is

a sliver of light.

Gabriel's spirits are elevated.

Magical thinking returns,

as it always does.

Perhaps,

he thinks,

perhaps.

The subways are running,

as are the buses

and the taxis

and the ferries

and the trucks.

The vehicles appear to move slower,

less frequently,

than they did before the pestilence arrived.

The roads are open,

as are the bridges

and the tunnels

and the highways

and the bus terminals

and the train stations

and the airports.

The transportation pathways and hubs are now emptier,

less congested,

more pleasant than before.

Goods and people flow not with the celerity of old,

but at a lesser speed that frustrates the modern consumer.

Anything short of immediate gratification has become

a disappointment,

a failure.

Networks transmit greater amounts of data

at faster and faster speeds.

(To what end,

Gabriel wonders.)

But perhaps the most welcome change is that time,

linear time,

has been restored.

Gone is the monolithic

void-like

mass of time

that cannot be sliced

or divided

or measured.

Gone is the melding of

hours

and days

and weeks

(and work weeks)

and months

and seasons

and years.

People can now,

for the first time since death arrived,

keep track of time.

Gabriel checks his watch

and sees that twelve days

and fourteen hours

and thirty-seven minutes

have passed since he saw

that sliver of light

in Sophie's window.

Sophie sits in her apartment with the blinds lowered,
except for four inches at the bottom.
She has remained alone in her apartment for the last three weeks
and has not made the bed.
Two things happened,
or didn't happen,
three weeks ago.
First,
a man who had been spending almost every night with her
turned out to be an incompatible partner.
(He winced when she talked at great length
about the beauty of her grandmother's home in Marrakech
and her grandfather's love of the poetry of Gibran Khalil Gibran.
He grimaced when Sophie pronounced foreign cities
as if she were a local
and not an American.
A bit pretentious,

he said,

which wounded her.

She replied that anglicizing a name for no good reason

is much worse than being pretentious.)

Three weeks ago they had an argument about music.

She loves vocal deep house music.

He finds the music to be monotonous

and derided her love of this genre.

He left after the argument and never returned.

On his way out

he said spiteful things,

the types of things that only men who hate women

say to women.

Second,

the daughter she placed for adoption as a baby

had just turned eighteen.

Sophie became depressed every year on her daughter's birthday.

She would typically spend a day or two in bed

and then recover from her sadness.

This year was different,

for the girl's eighteenth birthday meant that

she had become an adult,

that young woman now has the legal authority

to learn Sophie's identity
and to contact her biological mother if she wants.
The young woman has not contacted her.
Even though Sophie understands that it would be unlikely
for her daughter to reach out on the very day of her adulthood,
she is still crestfallen.
(Another layer of ambiguous loss.)
She is so crestfallen
that she has not left her apartment in three weeks
and has made no effort to connect with the outside world.
Other than her work,
which she now conducts entirely from home,
she has had almost no contact with anyone.
She does not look out the window,
to the streets below.
She does not return the calls of friends or family.
She does not wave the red flag,
or the white flag,
at Gabriel.
(She has waved the white flag to herself though.)
Her only non-work communication
is one that she fears was
neither seen,

nor understood.

She raised the blinds by four inches

with the hope that Gabriel might notice.

Sophie has endured similar dark times in the past.

(Gabriel is correct in his assumption that

she is prone to bouts of melancholy,

but he is wrong about several other things.

For instance she does not make a delicious savory pie

and she does not have beautiful penmanship.)

She has arisen from these prior dark times

through the most commonplace actions.

(Like Gabriel,

Sophie too once had an irritating therapist

who relied on pithy little sayings

and cutesy adages.

The therapist told her that

you can change a thought

by moving a muscle.)

Sophie thus resolves to take a shower

and make the bed

and put up a pot of fresh coffee

and go outside and walk around the block

and raise the blinds.

She will perform the most ordinary tasks

in an attempt to lift her depression.

She walks over to the blinds

and grabs the rope

and pulls down so that

the blinds rise up

four more inches.

Gabriel stands in his apartment and watches the blinds rise

by an additional four inches.

Perhaps,

he thinks,

perhaps.

But for a few holdovers
the city has returned fully to its pre-contagion state,
its natural cadence and chaos restored.
There is the occasional outlier who still wears a mask
and the mood is such that this cautious individual
may now be looked upon by some as
a lunatic
a fool
a germaphobe
an enemy of freedom
a follower
a sheep
a mindless drone.
This masked individual may in fact
be sick and concerned with protecting others
or immunocompromised and concerned with protecting himself
or exceedingly fearful given the loss of a loved one

or an eccentric who enjoys wearing masks
or a celebrity seeking to avoid attention
or a thief seeking to avoid identification
or an iconoclast
or someone who views those who refuse to wear masks as
the sheep.
Regardless,
people ride packed subway cars
and dine in crowded restaurants
and cram themselves into bars and cafes.
They hug and kiss and have sex with abandon.
They now live as if the contagion never happened.
Many have been liberated not just from the grip of the plague
but also from the grip of their former lives,
their conditioning,
their parochial thinking,
the muscle memory that had built up over decades.
For these people the contagion
has served as
a hard reboot.
Their operating systems have been reset.
Perhaps these survivors have come to view their lives,
their mortality,

from a new perspective.
Perhaps they now have a greater appreciation
for the finiteness of life
and the randomness of death
and the need to enjoy every moment.
(They have developed a rosier perspective
as a result of this plague.)
Or perhaps they now have a greater appreciation for
the finiteness of life
and the randomness of death
and they have come to believe that
that there is no meaning to life,
that everything means nothing,
that nothing means anything.
(They have become nihilists of sorts.
They just don't care anymore.)
Either way the result is similar.
These two groups have ended up in similar places.
There is of course another group,
one that has neither developed a newfound appreciation for life
nor developed a nihilistic yet liberating attitude.
With a certain acceptance grounded in experience
this group has merely picked up where things left off.

(Gabriel believes that he falls into this group.)
These people view the global contagion
and the deaths of tens of millions
and the restrictions on movement and freedom
and the economic pain
as nothing more than an inevitable interruption
in the flow of life,
one of so many over the centuries,
and one that will be repeated
over and over.
There will be another interruption one day,
they reason.
A global war.
An economic crisis.
Another pestilence.
The most painful ambiguous loss.
These people shrug their shoulders
and go about their business as they always have.
Gabriel sits at a café on the Upper West Side and observes life.
He watches people walk about in the sunshine
and enjoy a gentle breeze,
and he thinks about the last several years
and this new freedom.

He thinks about his life and whether there is anything
he wants to change.
He enjoys his career and would like to be more productive.
He resolves to improve the vessel that holds mementos
and that is inspired by contemporary French ceramics.
He thinks about his physical confinement,
about everyone's physical confinement,
over the past few years
and how he traveled infrequently in the years preceding.
He resolves to travel more,
to travel far and wide.
He is committed to his recovery
and would like to strengthen his ties to that community.
He resolves to attend more meetings
and to be of greater service to those in need.
He would like to have a healthy romantic relationship,
a partnership.
(He had a healthy romantic partnership with his former wife
but his drinking
and his cruel accusations
destroyed it.
He hates himself for destroying that partnership.
He has not forgiven himself,

even though she has

forgiven him.)

Gabriel looks across the street

and sees someone who looks familiar,

important even.

His heart races.

He rises to get a better look

and sees her stop at a shop window.

Her back is turned to him

but there is something about her hair

her posture and her bearing

that makes him think he knows this woman.

(The woman who makes the bed,

he thinks,

yes it must be.)

The woman turns so that she faces Gabriel.

She takes a step in his direction

and then another,

and it is then that he realizes

he does not know this woman.

He sits back down and continues to watch the people pass.

Having seen this woman,

this stranger,

his thoughts turn to Sophie.
He recalls the blinds being lifted several inches
and then another several inches.
He assumes that the man has continued to visit her,
that she is happy.
He assumes that she has formed a healthy romantic relationship,
a partnership,
with another human being.
He resolves again to try to form such a partnership.
He understands that to do so will require him to take certain risks,
the kind of risks that he has not taken since his wife left.
(Gabriel is so afraid of suffering another loss that he does not
go on the apps to meet women
or approach women at the gym
or ask friends to set him up.
He also does not ask women from the meetings on dates,
as he believes that to do so would entail
an increased level of risk
for both him and the woman.)
He scans the café and resolves to be more assertive.
A seat opens up next to him
and a woman sits down.
They make fleeting eye contact

and she removes a book from her bag.
She reads a book that is one of Gabriel's favorites.
The Twentieth Century Russian novel is about the devil
descending upon Moscow
and the havoc he wreaks.
Accompanying Satan is an enormous evil hilarious cat
named Behemoth.
Gabriel notices that the woman is nearing the end of the book.
He would like to speak with her about the book.
He considers his post-plague resolution to be more assertive,
to talk not just with women with the hope of forming
a romantic partnership,
but with people of all kinds,
with the hope of forming friendships
or acquaintanceships
or even short moments that,
despite their brevity,
have meaning.
He gathers his courage to address the woman.
He takes a sip of water to clear his throat.
Excuse me,
he says,
I saw you're reading *The Master and Margarita*,

one of my favorites.

The woman smiles and raises her hand,

palm facing Gabriel,

fingers straight up.

Not interested,

she says,

and returns to her book.

Gabriel gasps.

He experiences the pain of rejection.

A few moments of discomfort ensue

and he comes to appreciate the woman's firm boundaries,

how she articulates so clearly what she wants

and does not want.

(He admired the same confidence in his former wife.)

He nods politely.

He stands and leaves the café.

Slightly shaken by the woman's efficient rejection

Gabriel decides to go to a nearby meeting.

He walks over to the church,

to the church basement,

where he sees many friends

and other like-minded people.

He raises his hand at the meeting

and tells the story of the woman who deftly
and confidently
and unequivocally
said to him,
Not interested.
People at the meeting laugh.
They laugh because there can be great humor in embarrassment,
in particular the embarrassment of others,
and because,
for these hypersensitive
and perseverating
and often insecure people,
even the most minor embarrassment
can lead to relapse.
Laughter reduces the weight of embarrassment
and thus reduces the chance of relapse.
The Master and Margarita,
he says to the group.
What was I *thinking*?

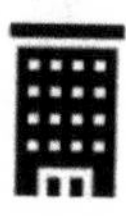

The two doctors carry their newborn baby into the apartment
for the first time.
They are joined by the parents of one man,
but not by the parents of the other.
(The taller of the two men is filled with such joy
that he does not think about
the disgust with which his parents treat him
and his marriage
and the fact that he has a child with another man.)
Gabriel smiles as he watches this growing family
and he raises a celebratory fist in their honor.
The two men carry their baby into the earth-toned nursery
and place her on the changing table.
They have no idea how to handle their own baby
or to change a diaper.
They are nervous.
Both of these men are physicians

and as part of their training
they have delivered several babies
and cared for many.
This training though has not prepared them
for the first few hours
of their own parenting.
They are flummoxed.
Together they remove the soiled diaper
and clumsily drop it to the floor.
They clean their daughter
and place a new diaper on her
(incorrectly)
and then another
(also incorrectly)
until they at last secure one to her.
They move her to the crib and place her on her back,
the baby monitor by her side.
They tap the mobile
and cause it to sway above her.
She watches the swaying mobile.
They step back and admire their child.
When they shut the light in the nursery and lower the blinds,
Gabriel turns his attention to the apartment of the socialite.

Her blinds have been lowered for weeks,
but today they are raised
and Gabriel can see people moving about the apartment.
There is a cleaning crew
and the woman's assistant too.
The assistant takes certain items from her bedroom
and tosses them into a garbage bag.
There are half-empty bottles of perfume
and undergarments
and old paperback books
and magazines
and pill bottles
and toiletries
and other items of little sentimental
or economic value.
The assistant strips the bed and places the bedding in the trash.
Photographs of the socialite with many of her friends
and acquaintances
and complete strangers
are removed from their frames and thrown in the trash,
and those frames that have any value
are placed carefully in a box.
Based upon the items being discarded by the assistant

Gabriel is confident that the woman has died.

He surmises that the socialite has died from loneliness,

which was caused by the cancellation of her social life,

which in turn was caused by the contagion.

(He is correct.)

Gabriel again considers the people he has been observing,

those whose lives he has witnessed,

those whose stories he has manufactured.

The socialite is dead.

One Mancunian is dead

and the other Mancunian

is either dead

or has moved away.

(He is in fact dead.)

The old man has moved Upstate with his daughter.

The two doctors have remained

and added a baby to their family.

Sophie has remained

and the only evidence of her presence is that,

on occasion,

her blinds move

a few inches.

Four have died or moved

and three have remained

and one child has been added.

Seven has thus been reduced to four.

Gabriel is disheartened by the math

and he wonders if this math is representative,

if it has been repeated

in other neighborhoods

throughout this city

and other cities

throughout the world.

Gabriel is excited about his work.

Not only has he designed

a beautiful and functional memento holder,

but he has been hired by a leading consumer products company

to design

a garlic press

and a paper towel holder

and a honey bottle.

(He is excited to design a bottle

that does not cause the honey to stick to the lid

or drip down the side.)

Gabriel finds it satisfying to elevate the most mundane items

into objects that possess

both beauty and function.

As Gabriel works on a design for the garlic press

he glances in the direction of Sophie's window

and is startled to see that her blinds are wide open,

that he can see into her bedroom again.
He rises and rather than stand visibly at the window,
he hides behind the drapes
like he did in the early days,
when asymmetry prevailed.
He watches Sophie as she makes the bed.
He looks for signs of the man who used to stay over
but he does not see any indication of his presence.
Sophie makes her bed with the precision of old.
She tucks the sheet into hospital corners
and tosses the pillows
and punches them
and then stacks them at the head of the bed.
She steps back and admires her work.
(Sophie has emerged from her depression,
which started when the man called her pretentious
because she pronounces foreign capitals
as they are meant to be pronounced,
and when her daughter's eighteenth birthday,
an ambiguous loss,
came and went.)
Gabriel thinks about the resolutions he has made,
and how,

The Master and Margarita notwithstanding,

he wishes to make new connections with new people.

Gabriel goes to his closet and removes the other half of the sheet

that he cut months ago,

when he asked Sophie if she was okay.

With a marker he writes

I'm Gabriel,

would you like to have coffee?

With the sheet in hand he hides behind the drapes.

He watches Sophie for several minutes as she tidies her room

and makes a cup of tea.

When she stands in front of her window

and enjoys the feeling of warmth

that emanates from the hot mug

and radiates into the flesh of her palms,

Gabriel steps out from behind the drapes.

He holds up the sheet.

I'm Gabriel,

would you like to have coffee?

At first she does not see him or the sign.

She gazes out the window,

to the street below.

Perhaps she is reflecting on another day passed.

Perhaps she is considering the quality of her life
or the quantity that remains.
Gabriel waves the sheet.
He hopes to catch her attention
and she soon sees him standing in the window frame
with a sheet in his hands.
Sophie squints as if trying to read the words.
Gabriel wonders if the words are too small.
(They are not.)
She puts the mug down on her dresser and stares at the sign.
She disappears behind the bedroom door
and Gabriel is sure that he has experienced another rejection.
He believes that a rejection in this context
would be entirely reasonable and prudent.
He believes that a reasonable and prudent woman
would reject him under these circumstances.
He is about to drop the sheet to the floor when Sophie reappears.
With her glasses on
she stands in front of the window
and raises her right arm.
In her hand she holds the red flag
that her friend gave her as a reminder to avoid
unsuitable partners.

Sophie waves the flag in the window.

Gabriel sees the flag being waved.

He now understands what this red flag means.

He understands that

he may be the red flag,

that he is the danger to be avoided.

She is reasonable and prudent,

he thinks.

He drops the sheet to the floor

and prepares to return to his sketches.

(He will share this rejection too in the meeting.

On the heels of *The Master and Margarita* rejection,

he anticipates even more uproarious laughter

from his fellow drunks.)

He looks again and sees that Sophie is no longer holding

the red flag.

Instead she smiles and gives him a thumbs-up sign.

She then holds up all ten fingers

and then taps her watch

and points downward,

to the street.

Stunned,

Gabriel gives her a thumbs-up sign.

He holds up all ten fingers

and then taps his watch

and points downward,

to the street.

In ten minutes

Gabriel and Sophie,

who have been watching each other for months

in the midst of this plague,

sometimes symmetrically

and sometimes asymmetrically,

will meet on the street

and walk

and drink coffee together.

Gabriel has ten minutes to get ready.
He brushes his teeth
and combs his hair
and puts on a nice shirt
and a sweater that he has been told
complements his physique.
He eschews his old sneakers
in favor of suede boots
that give him an extra inch.
He looks in the mirror.
He checks his watch and sees that he has four minutes to spare.
On the way out he glances down to the Mancunians' apartment,
which has been vacant for months.
Gabriel watches as a young man,
a new tenant,
walks around the terrace.
The young man picks up a few dead rose petals,

detritus left by the Mancunians.

The man has placed new planters along the edge of the terrace.

The planters contain boxwoods and Japanese pines.

The young man lifts the hose and waters the plants.

He stands back and examines his work.

His dog,

a Border terrier,

darts out onto the terrace,

lifts his leg

and pees on one of the Japanese pines.

The man does not have the heart to scold the dog,

who is curious and excited

by his new home.

As Gabriel walks to the elevator

he continues to tell a story about this young man,

to manufacture a story about this stranger.

(He is from the Midwest,

from Cleveland perhaps,

and has recently graduated from college.

He works at an investment bank

or a tech company.

He loves jazz

and kebabs

and poetry slams.)

As Gabriel constructs a tale about this human being,
as he begins to do what he has done to the others,
he experiences a feeling of nausea,
a soul sickness of sorts.
He realizes that he no longer is invigorated
by the creation of a story.
The fabrication of a complete stranger
saddens him,
and makes him think that a rich fantasy life can be both
a blessing and a curse.
(During the epidemic Gabriel's rich fantasy life was a blessing,
for it allowed him to pass time
when time had ceased to be linear,
but it is now a curse,
for it distracts him from what is going on in the world
and separates him from reality,
from the business of living.)
The elevator doors open and Gabriel steps out into the lobby.
He steps outside and walks across the street,
to Sophie's building.
He is nervous.
He crosses the street
and sees Sophie standing in front of her building.
She is slightly taller than he realized,

with finer features and a profile that makes him think of
the *Portrait of Madame X.*
He approaches her and extends his hand.
She looks at his face
and then at his unsteady hand.
She shakes it,
squeezes it,
stabilizes it.
Nice to meet you,
she says.
I've been calling you Drape Guy to my friends.
Gabriel bites his lower lip in shame.
Close,
he says,
it's Gabriel.
And I've been calling you Sophie.
She rolls her eyes.
Close too,
she says,
scary close.
It's Sandrine,
both French with an S.
The two release hands and begin to walk west,
toward Riverside Park.

On the way they stop at a café and pick up coffee to go.

They are both uncomfortable and struggle to make

even superficial conversation.

These two people,

who have been watching each other for months,

who have observed so many intimate domestic moments,

who have in some way together survived a near extinction event,

these two people cannot speak.

They struggle to connect.

When they reach the entrance to the park she asks,

How does this work.

(The silence has become so uncomfortable

that she must acknowledge it.)

He shrugs his shoulders.

I don't know,

he says,

I think we just keep walking until someone speaks.

Okay,

she says,

and they stroll through the park in awkward silence.

Sandrine thinks about the red flag that her friend gave her

as a reminder to avoid unsuitable partners,

and the white flag to remind her when it's time to give up,

to surrender.

(Through surrender there is strength.)

Gabriel loves this park.

When he strolls up and down the tree-lined boulevard

he imagines himself to be a flâneur of sorts,

a carefree stroller.

(Gabriel is in fact almost never carefree.)

Shall we sit down,

he asks,

pointing to a bench that looks out over the river.

They sit in silence and watch the water.

After a few minutes Gabriel says something.

He regrets the question

while he asks the question.

Did it bother you when I watched you?

Watched you make the bed?

Sandrine follows a tugboat as it moves downriver.

No,

she says without further explanation.

Gabriel nods,

an almost indiscernible drop and raise of his head.

They watch the river together.

A helicopter buzzes overhead on its way to New Jersey.

The bridge stands guard to the north.

A flock of birds moves west to east,

over their heads.

They sit quietly,

in stillness.

Sandrine glances to her right,

to Gabriel.

She notes his shaking left hand that rests on his thigh.

He is a nervous sort,

she thinks.

Something must have happened to him,

something terrible.

Sandrine reaches over

and holds his hand.

She stops his hand from shaking.

They watch the river.

They do not speak.

Minutes pass the way minutes should pass.

They are in no rush.

Time is linear.

Time is again linear.

A family of four has moved into the socialite's apartment.
Gabriel has seen these people but has made a purposeful effort
not to form an opinion about them,
not to construct a story about them,
not to project on to them certain qualities
or traits
or interests.
He has resolved,
whenever possible,
to avoid the soul sickness of fantasy.
What he has done though is make an updated calculation
about net gains and net losses.
With the loss of the Mancunians
and the socialite
and the old man
and with the addition of the doctors' baby girl,
seven had been reduced to four.

And with the addition of the young man who has taken over
the Mancunians' apartment
and the family of four that has moved into the socialite's place,
four has been increased to nine.
What once was seven is now nine.
The tableau vivant that Gabriel created has experienced
a net gain of two.
Gabriel is heartened by the math
and he wonders if this math is representative,
if it has been repeated
throughout this city
and other cities
around the world.
Gabriel can no longer see Sandrine in her apartment
and she can no longer see him.
They have each decided to keep their blinds lowered
in order to enforce symmetry.
Now that they have met each other,
now that they have held hands
and watched the river in silence,
even the remote possibility of asymmetry
is intolerable to both of them.
At seven o'clock each evening,

at the precise moment that the residents of this city
once leaned from their windows
and banged their pots
and clapped their hands
and screamed
and howled
and clapped
and played their kazoos
(Gabriel still wonders how the socialite came to own a kazoo),
Gabriel and Sandrine meet in front of her building
and go for a walk.
They share very little with each other,
except for comfort
and companionship.
They say a few words
but have avoided any sustained or deep conversation.
When they walk
Sandrine often slips her hand under Gabriel's arm.
Sometimes Gabriel holds her hand.
(She notices that his hands no longer tremble.)
Tonight they walk south toward Lincoln Center.
As they walk
a large crowd of people pours out of a church.

Gabriel is taken aback,

as they are people from his meeting.

They greet him with enthusiasm and warmth.

They are happy to see him.

Dozens of people wave and smile.

A few men give him pats on the back.

(A Welshman screams,

There goes the hatchet man.

Knowing nothing of Gabriel's award-winning axe design

Sandrine is confused by this ominous greeting.)

One of the elderly women who protects the young women

gives him a wink as if to say,

I approve of your date.

The crowd passes

and Gabriel and Sandrine continue their silent walk.

After a few blocks she asks,

Anything you want to tell me about those people,

how you know them.

He pauses and considers his response.

Drunks,

he says.

Addicts too.

She thinks about his response.

Okay,

she says.

She understands what this means.

Without knowing the details,

without wanting to know the details at this time,

she accepts this part of him.

(Her friend would tell her that she is ignoring

an obvious red flag.)

She squeezes his elbow

and they keep walking.

Gabriel and Sandrine sit on a bench in Central Park.

There is a playground nearby

and they can hear the children yelling.

Do you have kids,

he asks.

(He is confident that she does not

because he has never seen a child in her apartment.

Still,

he asks the question.)

Did once,

she says,

for a few minutes.

He pauses to consider her answer and his possible response.

He fears that to ask her what happened to her child

might be too personal.

Me too,

he says,

for a few years.

She pauses to consider her response.

She too fears that to ask him what happened to his child

might be too personal.

Neither of them feels the need to know more at the moment.

They sit on the bench

and listen to the children play

and watch the people pass by.

Sandrine and Gabriel keep their blinds up only when
the other is out of town
or at work
or otherwise away from the apartment.
(They require symmetry
but also seek light and views
when the opportunity presents.)
Today Sandrine is at her office
so Gabriel's blinds are raised.
(All he knows about her job
is that she works for a not-for-profit organization
and that she no longer works from home all week.
She now goes into the office on Tuesdays,
Wednesdays
and Thursdays
and works from home on Mondays and Fridays.
Gabriel wonders how these new work arrangements might impact

the math of the city,

the net gains and net losses.

He believes that there are sound arguments for both,

for net gains or net losses.)

He looks out his window and is surprised to see movement

in the old man's apartment.

The man left long ago to live with his daughter Upstate

and Gabriel has not seen him since.

The front door opens

and the old man and his daughter enter.

They drop their bags in the foyer and look around the apartment.

The man runs his finger across the wood of his old desk.

He appears to reflect on something from the past,

something that causes an ache,

or perhaps he simply reconnects with a familiar object.

The daughter is moved by the look on her father's face.

She sees the look of someone who has returned home.

She opens the windows to allow the air to enter.

She slaps the sofa cushions

and watches the clouds of dust rise and rotate.

The man opens his cupboards to see what remains.

There are a few jars of spaghetti sauce and a box of pasta.

He takes out the copper pot and boils water for the pasta,

for both of them.

The daughter approaches him

and gives him a hug and a kiss on the cheek.

The many months they spent alone together in the country

have changed her,

softened her.

She has developed an admiration for her father's self-sufficiency,

for the care with which he treated her mother,

for the challenges he faced in his career,

how he never achieved his potential

and how he never became bitter

because he failed to achieve his potential.

She has come to understand the disappointment,

the pain,

that her distance has caused.

She has not yet figured out why she became so distant,

why she visited him so infrequently.

She has resolved to make amends to him

through her actions.

She reasons that while the wasted years cannot be recovered

she can take comfort

that there is still some time left.

(As it relates solely to her relationship with her father

she is thankful for the contagion.)

She turns on the music that he loves.

(The Doobie Brothers.)

She takes off her shoes and reads a book on the couch.

She pulls a blanket up over her legs.

She feels settled,

secure.

She was raised in this apartment

and she too bears the look of someone who has returned home.

From the kitchen the old man glances at his daughter,

his only child.

In this light,

and from this angle,

she looks just like her mother.

Sandrine and Gabriel sit at a table at a Thai restaurant
on the Upper West Side.
There is an affordable lunch special that they have come to enjoy.
(The lunch is affordable only by the standards of this
unaffordable city.)
Recently they have begun to share more details
about each other's lives.
Gabriel has discussed his drinking
and his recovery
and his award-winning axe.
(The Welshman's hatchet-man quip
now makes sense to Sandrine.)
He revealed that his daughter died when she was fifteen,
but has not yet gone into detail about her death.
He revealed that he was divorced,
but has not yet gone into detail about the demise of his marriage.
Sandrine respects his boundaries.

There is no rush,

she thinks,

as he discloses and then closes.

She has discussed her upbringing.

She comes from a loving family,

from a working-class neighborhood in north Philly.

She also has discussed her proclivity to become involved with unsuitable partners.

They sit at the restaurant

and eat Thai food

and drink jasmine tea.

Gabriel notices how she holds the teacup in her palms

and how she enjoys the emanating warmth.

He recalls seeing her drink like this in her window.

Without context Gabriel asks her if she enjoys

tart fruits or Nineteenth Century Russian literature.

She straightens up in her seat.

No to the former

and yes but rarely to the latter,

she says.

Why do you ask?

No reason,

he replies.

(He was wrong about many of the things he projected on to her.

He is surprised that she does not like tart fruits.)

Today Sandrine discusses her love for travel.

She names several places that she has travelled to

and which she found fascinating

or beautiful

or historical

or just plain fun.

There's Milano

and Roma

and Paris

and Montevideo

and Wien

to name a few she says.

Gabriel notices how she pronounces these international cities

as if she is a native.

He finds it unusual for an American to pronounce these cities

as she does,

but also entirely logical.

For the first time he thinks about the absurdity of using

three syllables to say

Vienna

when the single syllable of

Wien

would be more efficient.

He admires Sandrine's independence of thought.

(The same traits that offend one person

often attract another.)

They eat their pad khing and red curry.

They have become comfortable enough that they sometimes

share their food.

I had a daughter too,

she says before pulling a shrimp from the curry.

Gabriel puts down his chopsticks out of respect for her.

I was fifteen

and we had no money

and my parents were ashamed

and that's what I did.

I think it was the right decision.

There's no way I could take care of her,

no way my parents could either.

Gabriel considers his response.

Despite his calculation that a question at this moment

presents a greater risk than silence,

Gabriel asks,

Is it hard for you,

now I mean.

She shifts in her seat.

(He thinks about the many times when a well-intentioned person

said the wrong thing to him.)

It is from time to time,

she says.

(Her response indicates that he has not said

the wrong thing.)

Just a few weeks ago it was her eighteenth birthday.

That was a big one.

Not just because it's a milestone

but also because now she can contact me if she wants.

So maybe it's even harder than it was for all these years.

Before I had no chance of seeing her

but now I guess I do.

Seems like sometimes you can know too much

and too little

at the same time,

she says.

(Sandrine is haunted by both

regret and hope.

The chance that she might one day see her daughter again

makes her pain more acute.

The gravity of her ambiguous loss
has thus been counterintuitively magnified
by the possibility of healing that same loss.)
Gabriel reaches across the table and holds her hand.
Now it is her hand that shakes.
(They have never kissed each other.
Their infrequent physical contact has been limited to
the touching
and holding
and sometimes interlocking
of hands.)
They eat in silence,
in the most comfortable silence.
They reach across the table and snatch food
from the other's plate.
A rice noodle,
a piece of broccoli,
a slice of ginger.
For no reason other than habit
Gabriel rubs two chopsticks against each other
as if he is trying to start a fire.
Sandrine folds an empty sugar packet in half
and then half again,

and then unfolds it.

They are in no hurry to go anywhere

or do anything

or say anything.

Sandrine waves to the waiter

and asks for another pot of tea,

for two.

They are enjoying the passage of time,

the slow

and easy

and sometimes dreamy

linearity of time.

Gabriel steps into his apartment after the Thai lunch.

His home seems to have taken on a different appearance,

a different feel,

since the world reopened.

He looks to the floor,

to the thin crack in the tile

where the EMT dropped an oxygen tank

while she was trying to save their daughter.

He stands on the precise spot where she died.

Sometimes he will lie down on the tile floor,

on this very spot,

and take a short nap.

He likes to do this when the weather is hot

and the tiles are cool.

He peers into his closet and sees at the very end

two winter coats once owned by his former wife.

She left them in haste on her way out.

He tried to return them

but she showed little interest.

He later thought that he should donate them to the clothing drive

but he never did.

Gabriel has long believed that

the chipped tile

and the winter coats

and the frayed blanket

and the treasured mementos

that he stores in the shoebox,

all give him comfort

and allow him to keep going,

forward.

(He is incorrect,

as their presence has the opposite effect.

Their presence anchors him to the past.

Their presence causes suffering and

strips time of its forward linearity.)

Gabriel thinks about these connections to his past.

He thinks about the new connections he hopes to make,

about Sandrine

and about the new industrial design projects

he has been working on.

He glances again at the cracked tile on the floor
and verges on a decision,
one that he has avoided making on or around
this same date
for the past six years.
His lease expires at the end of the month.
and he decides that he will not renew it.
He will instead move out and find another place to live
and he will leave as much behind as possible.
Perhaps he will move to another city
or to the mountains
or the beach
or another country.
Perhaps he will stay in New York
and move to a neighborhood where he has never lived.
(The East Village appeals to him,
as does Jackson Heights in Queens.)
Perhaps he will travel the world,
like he once did in his youth.
He looks out his window and considers what it would feel like
to no longer have this view,
this perspective,
a window into the lives of others.

(Across the way
the old man and his daughter
make lunch together.)
Gabriel sits down at his desk
and takes out his drawings of a garlic press
and a paper towel holder
and a honey bottle
and a vessel to hold mementos.
He assesses the vessel,
with its organic ceramic design
and its small compartments inside.
The vessel to him now represents the past.
(For Gabriel the past is not over
but it is almost over.)
He tears up the sketch of the vessel and throws it in the bin.
He turns to the garlic press
and admires his creation.
He believes that he has accomplished
what many have attempted to accomplish
but that few have.
He has designed a press in which the garlic,
the skin of the garlic,
does not stick to the device.

(He has included an ingenious little button
that pushes the skin away
from the surface of the press.)
He is pleased.
He believes that he has been unlocked in many ways,
creative and otherwise.
He looks over to Sandrine's apartment
and sees that she too returns home from their lunch.
He watches as she drops her keys on the table
and kicks off her shoes
and frees her hair.
Committed to a symmetry that has become sacred,
he lowers his blinds.

Gabriel stands in his empty apartment on the last day of his lease.
He is required to leave the place broom clean
but he would like the new tenants,
a young couple from France,
to walk into an immaculate apartment.
He scrubs the surfaces and fixtures in the kitchen and bathroom.
He mops the wood floors with a pine-scented soap
and wipes the windows clean.
With an old toothbrush he removes the dirt that has gathered
in the tiny crack in the floor tile.
In the refrigerator
he leaves for the new tenants
a bottle of prosecco.
(As someone who does not drink
he always feels odd giving alcohol as a gift.)
Next to the bottle he leaves a note.
May this home bring you as much joy as it brought me.

Gabriel is not being disingenuous.

While the apartment has been the site of his greatest losses,

it has also been home to his most joyous experiences.

He walks to the foyer

and kneels down

and runs his fingers over

the tiny crack in the tile.

He stands with full acceptance that his time here is done.

(To Gabriel the crack represents time.)

There are two small bags near the door.

He has rid himself of everything

except for the contents of these two bags,

which contain only those few items that he considers essential.

He steps out of the apartment,

bags in hand,

and closes the door behind him.

He does not consider the end of his tenure in this apartment

to be a loss,

ambiguous or otherwise.

He considers the end to be an essential element,

a foundational element,

of Possibility.

As he walks to the elevator

he does the math,

calculating net losses

and net gains.

With the loss of the Mancunians

and the socialite

and the old man

and with the addition of the doctors' baby girl,

seven had been reduced to four.

With the addition of the young man

who moved into the Mancunians' apartment

and the family of four that moved into the socialite's place,

four had increased to nine.

And with the addition of the young couple from France

nine has been increased to eleven.

(He does not yet realize that his calculation

is flawed,

incomplete.)

The tableau vivant that Gabriel observed

and narrated

and inhabited

has now expanded.

Possibility, he thinks.

Gabriel meets Sandrine for a walk.

He did not tell her that he was moving.

(He feared telling her.)

As they walk down Columbus

he tells her that he is moving,

that he has already moved.

She hides her disappointment

that he did not tell her in advance

and that he has moved.

Where are you going,

she asks.

Not sure yet,

he says.

Maybe Milano

or Roma

or Paris

or Montevideo

or Wien.

He pronounces these cities as if he is a local.

Gabriel mocks her in the way that we mock

the people we adore.

Because he is leaving though,

Sandrine does not find it funny.

(Adoring mockery works only when the adored

feels secure in the relationship.)

Or maybe I'll just go downtown,

he says.

I understand,

she replies,

I understand.

I'm disappointed,

she continues,

failing to hide

her disappointment.

Stay in touch,

she asks,

a command disguised

as a question.

Stay in touch,

he assures her.

Their physical contact has been limited to their hands
but now they hug,
long and tight.
There is something desperate about the way that they hug,
as if a cloudy and potent fear
has arisen in each of them.
They separate and take a few moments to commit to memory
the features of the other's face
and then Gabriel lifts his bags and walks away.
Sandrine returns to her apartment.
She raises the blinds
and looks at the sky
and the street below
She considers the quality of her life
and the quantity that might remain.
On the street below she watches as Gabriel tries to hail a cab.
Several drive right past him
and she can feel his frustration.
A taxi stops
and he places his two bags in the trunk.
He gets inside the car
and is gone.
A half hour later

Sandrine's friend comes over to provide comfort.
(Sandrine had told her about Gabriel
and the friend had reminded her about red flags.)
The two friends share a bottle of wine
and listen to music
and talk about relationships.
Sandrine describes how Gabriel hugged her
with something that felt like desperation
and how she did the same to him.
She asks her friend what that might mean.
The friend shakes her head
in disapproval
and picks up the red flag
and waves it dramatically.
Sandrine tries to pull the red flag out of her friend's hand
but her friend resists
and they struggle for the flag
and then fall to the sofa
and laugh.
(The French couple enjoys their first hour
in Gabriel's old apartment.
They toast their good fortune
and drink the prosecco that Gabriel left for them.

They are grateful for the alcohol
and the kind note.
As they drink
they watch two women in an apartment across the street
struggle furiously to gain possession
of a small red flag.
The French couple are confused by what they see.
Americans,
they think.)

Six months have passed since Gabriel

last ran his fingertips over the tiny crack in the floor tile

and moved out of his apartment

and said an awkward goodbye to Sandrine

on the sidewalk.

During these six months

he lives a global and itinerant life,

spending eight weeks in each of Cartagena

and Wien

and Nairobi.

He finds that while time is linear in all of these places

the speed of linear time varies

from place to place.

Cartagena moves slowest,

the summer afternoons in particular,

and Nairobi moves fastest.

The time in Wien moves right in the middle

and without variation.

Regardless of season

the time in Wien moves

like a metronome.

(Tick tock

tick tock

tick tock.)

In each of these cities

Gabriel attends meetings

and encounters like-minded people

who share a similar affliction

and who possess many common personality traits.

These people,

like him,

are prone to peculiar

and often self-destructive

ways of thinking and behaving.

They often

ruminate over the past

and descend into self-pity

and resist change

and are overly sensitive to criticism

and struggle to form true partnerships

with other people
and generally underachieve in their lives.
(Whether these traits
are the symptom or the cause is unclear.
What is clear to Gabriel
is that most of these people,
despite their character traits,
are trying to get better.)
The frequent change of environment has
a dislodging effect on Gabriel's way of thinking.
During his long stay in Cartagena,
when he sits on a bench in Plaza Fernández de Madrid
and enjoys the chorus of children playing
and thinks of García Márquez and the ravages of cholera
and watches the world swirl wildly around him,
he comes to understand that perhaps
he is not as indifferent to the contagion
as he once thought,
that he is not like those people
who shrug their shoulders
and go about their business as they always have.
Perhaps he is,
to his great surprise,

one of those who are liberated

not just from the grip of pestilence

but also from the grip of their former lives,

their conditioning,

their parochial thinking,

the muscle memory that has built up over decades.

Perhaps the contagion

has served as

a hard reboot,

allowing him to let go of the past in ways that had once seemed impossible.

After six months of travel

Gabriel finds a new home.

(After months of travel

he has settled down.)

In this new home

he has none of his old furniture

or artwork

or dishes

or pots and pans

or plants

or rugs.

From his old apartment

he has taken only

some clothing

and a few books

and the baby blanket

and his daughter's first tooth

and the rose petals

and the baseball card

and the expired passports

and the old wedding ring

and the masonry from jail

and the piece of his childhood tree house

and his daughter's bracelet.

(Gabriel now embraces change

but still has one foot in the past.)

Gabriel stores these cherished items

not in a vessel inspired by French ceramics

but in an old shoebox,

which he has come to believe

is a perfect industrial design

that cannot be improved upon.

In this new home he has a tidy workspace,

a small wooden desk under a window

with a southern exposure.

It is here that he works

and reads

and drinks tea

and enjoys the passage of time,

the slow

and easy

and sometimes dreamy

linearity of time.

In this home he experiences a shift in perspective,

west to east.

He sees things differently than he did before,

from a different angle.

Gabriel sits at his desk and sketches in his pad.

He draws not his latest industrial design,

but something else,

something distant

and ethereal

and abstract.

He pauses to look around his home.

From the desk he can see into the bedroom.

There,

a woman walks around the bed.

She tucks the sheet into hospital corners,

tosses the pillows

and punches them

and then stacks them at the head of the bed.

Need any help,

Gabriel asks.

The woman turns to look at him.

I got it,

Sandrine replies.

The pain of possibility continues to haunt her.

The possibility that her daughter might contact her,

or might not contact her,

exacerbates her ambiguous loss.

The possibility that her daughter might be unhappy

exacerbates her loss.

The possibility that her daughter might not even be alive

exacerbates her loss.

And so on

and so on.

The unresolved is

gaping,

exposed.

In the partnership that has developed

between Gabriel and Sandrine,

her ambiguous loss
has the same standing,
the same importance,
the same impact,
as his unambiguous loss.
Her pain is as real as his,
and the fact that her pain is as real as his
helps her better tolerate the pain.
Sandrine finishes making the bed.
She sits on a chair next to Gabriel.
They look out the window.
They look into Gabriel's old apartment
and see the French couple inside.
They watch these two people
prepare a meal
and set the table
and dim the overhead lamp
and light candles.
These people turn on music,
one of their favorite songs by Serge Gainsbourg,
and meet in the center of Gabriel's old living room
and embrace
and dance to the music,

swaying.

When the song is over

they sit down at the table

and toast their good fortune

and enjoy their entrecôte.

(The French couple does the same things,

cooking

and embracing

and dancing

and toasting,

that Gabriel and his former wife did

when they first moved into this very home.)

Sandrine and Gabriel hold hands.

A pearly milky twilight

pours into their apartment

from some magical

and distant

and unknown place.

Gabriel eyes a house plant in the corner of the room.

A small red flag

and a small white flag

stick out of the dirt in the planter.

(They have been kept in this place since Sandrine

wrestled the red flag from her friend's fist.)

What are those flags for,

Gabriel asks.

(He thinks back to the time when he hid behind the drapes,

when she waved the red flag in his direction.)

Sandrine stands and removes the flags from the planter.

She waves the red one above her head.

To remind me to avoid people like you,

she says.

(She mocks him in the way that we mock

the people we adore.)

Prudent,

he replies.

She waves the white flag above her head.

And this one reminds me to surrender,

she says,

to let go of my fear.

She pauses.

My fear of people like you.

Gabriel smiles.

Less prudent,

he says.

He turns and admires a red hawk

as it glides past the window
in full extension.
He stands.
He scans the surrounding buildings
and considers the possibility,
the probability,
that others apply to him and Sandrine
the same level of asymmetry
that he once applied
to the people he observed.
He has come to accept asymmetry
as a natural consequence of living in this city,
an unavoidable dynamic in which
certain rights are surrendered
in exchange for the numerous benefits
of population density.
The urban tradeoff,
as Gabriel's wife once called it.
From the apartment below
he hears the old man's television blaring
and it occurs to him that,
since he returned to the city,
since he moved in with Sandrine,

the math has changed.

Eleven is now

twelve.

For the first time in his calculation

of net gains and net losses,

he has included himself

in the tableau of his creation.

(Life has descended

upon the city.)

He watches Sandrine,

in profile,

as she sits at the desk

and opens the mail.

With a hammered bronze letter opener

that Gabriel recently designed,

she slices an envelope

and removes a letter.

At the top of the letter is a government seal,

one that is familiar to her.

By instinct she reaches for her neck,

for her necklace.

She rubs the gold pendant

on which is inscribed an important date.

She reads the letter,

her hands shaking.

Gabriel takes a step toward her.

She looks up to him.

Her eyes water

and her jaw tightens

and her breathing accelerates.

She extends the letter to Gabriel.

(He takes a step closer.)

They have survived the plague.

(He takes the letter.)

They have made it through.

(He reads the letter.)

She tugs at her right ear.

With some difficulty

she stands.

Gabriel and Sandrine embrace each other.

They cry.

They have been altered.

They have been redeemed.

They have been resurrected

through

a plague of mercies.

Printed in the USA
CPSIA information can be obtained
at www.ICGtesting.com
JSHW080919110823
46255JS00020B/27

9 781733 258562